Dorothy Allen Mundy

S0-EPR-483

DANGER SIGNAL

By Phyllis Bottome

PRIVATE WORLDS

THE MORTAL STORM

DANGER SIGNAL

Danger Signal

PHYLLIS BOTTOME

Little, Brown and Company · Boston
1939

COPYRIGHT 1939, BY PHYLLIS FORBES-DENNIS

ALL RIGHTS RESERVED, INCLUDING THE RIGHT
TO REPRODUCE THIS BOOK OR PORTIONS
THEREOF IN ANY FORM

Published January 1939
Reprinted January 1939

PRINTED IN THE UNITED STATES OF AMERICA

To my friend

ALEXANDRA ADLER, M.D.

'I think affliction may subdue the cheek,
But not take in the mind.'
SHAKESPEARE: *A Winter's Tale.*

DANGER SIGNAL

Chapter 1

WHEN Hilda Fenchurch heard the familiar jarring whiz of the electric bell, she lifted her heavy-lidded eyes sullenly from her typewriter, and stared fiercely at the glass partition between her and the outer doorway, saying to herself, "If this is another of them, I'll go mad!"

The intruder from the outer world at least knew her own mind. She came in solidly after Harry the office boy had announced her, without dithering; nor did she begin to speak until Hilda had finished typing out her last sentence.

When she said "Good afternoon," Hilda guessed that she was a foreigner and thought with a sinking heart: "She'll dictate worse than any of them — if she wants to dictate; and if I have to copy her stuff, I'll have to learn the alphabet all over again!"

It was a mercy, however, that her customer was another woman. Hilda wouldn't have to keep comparing her to Ronnie, nor would she have to exert herself to cajole shy, or to repress forward, specimens of manhood. Other women were neither shy nor facetious, thank God, though they were often ruder than men, and usually more exacting. However, Hilda did not have red hair, and thick eyebrows that met across her nose, for nothing. Domineering women had better not try domineering over her in her own office! She might, of course, have plucked her eyebrows and made herself look like one of those slapped cats on the screen, but she had preferred to leave her eyebrows thick so that they took off from the rather large size of her nose; besides, other things being equal, Hilda liked looking natural.

"I should be obliged if you would type from my dictation some notes for a lecture that I am giving to-night," her visitor said in a low clear voice; her English was a shade more correct than usual, and Hilda found her surprisingly easy to understand.

Her new customer was stockily built, neither young nor old; she might still be in her early thirties, but she would not look very different when she was fifty. Her skin had the transparent clarity of a child's; her eyes rested on Hilda without any attempt to attract her attention, and without the shadow of a subterfuge. She seemed to have nothing to hide, and nothing to find. A curious look, Hilda thought, as if it would not have made much difference to her, personally, if Hilda had been either a black beetle or an archangel.

When her customer pushed back her hat, Hilda saw that her hair was red, rather a deeper shade than Hilda's own, quite straight and swept back in a solid mass from a broad, smooth brow. She did not smile at all, until after Hilda had agreed to take her work, but when she did smile, Hilda at once realized that she was not more than thirty.

It was a sweet, engaging smile, not the kind Hilda was used to, from customers. Customers, when they smiled at Hilda at all, generally did so because they wanted their work done for less money than they had any right to expect.

This one smiled because she was pleased that Hilda was willing to do her work; and thought, or gave Hilda the impression that she thought, that Hilda was particularly competent to do it.

"*I* could afford to be nice too," Hilda told herself sullenly, ducking her head down towards the typewriter to avoid having to smile back, "if I made pots of money lecturing, and people *had* to listen to me whether they liked it or not – and there wasn't any Ronnie!"

With an expert flip of her fingers, Hilda drew her carbons and flimsies together, and slipped them firmly and evenly under her roller. She did not look as if her heart were crying "Ah, Ronnie! Ronnie!"

She had got that lump in her throat again though, and it took some time swallowing it. That was the worst of the end of the summer, you felt the heat more and got hysterical; the rest of the year was much easier.

"If I go too fast, you will please stop me," her customer said and began to dictate. She did not raise her voice; she did not hurry; she never altered a phrase; so that Hilda found, in spite of her foreign accent, that she had never taken an easier dictation. The words slipped into Hilda's mind with the smoothness of cream. The subject was funny, Hilda thought. It was all about what you could do with your life, if your mind were trained to understand what you were really up to. Rather an interesting subject, Hilda told herself grimly, since she was training her own mind now, in a direction it had never been up to, before.

When Hilda came to psychological or medical terms, the foreign woman spelt them out, otherwise she offered Hilda no suggestions whatever.

Hilda liked being left to do her own work in her own way, and she did it very well, or she would not have been able to run an office of her own, however small – sharing the boy Harry with the Registry Office next door, but doing the work itself single-handed, at twenty-six; and earning from two to five pounds a week, by it.

Almost all her customers *did* make suggestions to Hilda about how she should do her work, because, Hilda grimly reminded herself, everyone who paid you money expected either to show off to you, or to interfere with you; or else they did both. This queer woman did neither, she seemed not to notice what Hilda did, and queerer still, not to notice what she herself did. She just went steadily on, until she had finished.

Then she looked at her watch, and said: "I have no more time, and I had meant to dictate two letters to you. Will you be so kind as to copy them instead? I will sign my name at the bottom of the paper you will use, and I should be grateful if you would post them on your way home."

Hilda was just about to say "It's not my job to post customers' letters!" but she bit the words back. After all, why should she not post them for this foreign lady, who perhaps did not know her way about? It was not as if Hilda would have to go out of her way in order to post them.

Her customer produced stamps, paid without comment what Hilda had asked, and then rose to her feet.

Once more Hilda found herself meeting those clear light eyes, neither blue nor grey. To her own surprise, Hilda heard herself saying: "Where is your lecture? I should like to hear it."

The lady promptly took out a card and wrote on it. "This," she said, "will give you free entrance. I am lecturing in Conway Hall. The lecture is at eight o'clock."

After she had gone, Hilda read her name – "*Doktor Elena Silla. Nervenarzt.*" Whatever that might mean. Beneath this was the name of a foreign hospital; and under that again "Prague."

Hilda sat down once more, and wrote the two letters. One was to the chief doctor of a pathological laboratory. His name was Manning Foster, and Dr. Silla regretted that she would be unable to see-over his Laboratory or to meet him, and his colleagues, the following morning, as she was leaving a day earlier than she had expected.

The other letter was to a friend. She seemed to mind not seeing this friend again, Hilda thought, though she did not carry on about it. She only said

"I'm sorry." It was funny, Hilda thought, that she should take the slightest interest in anything Dr. Silla felt.

"Why do I care," she asked herself bitterly, "*how* she feels saying good-bye to her probably potty, high-brow friend? Even my own family don't seem to matter to me much more than flies on the ceiling nowadays! I don't really care if the whole world gets smashed up, and goes to hell its own way, while I'm being twisted to death myself, by Ronnie!

"God in Heaven, how I hate him! Turning me down as if I were a snipped-off hair! And for Annie too! Curse him! Curse him! Couldn't he even leave my little sister alone?"

The worst of it was, that Annie was not just a fly on the ceiling to Hilda, she was half Hilda's life. You could not so easily wipe out of your mind some-one you had nursed when she was ill, – and Annie was always being ill, – whose battles you had always fought, whose happiness you had put before your own! Why had Annie had to have that long break-down and go abroad just this last year? And why should Hilda choose this same year to fall so desper-ately and irretrievably in love with Ronnie?

It had all fitted in with the dispatch and clarity of a nightmare.

Annie's room was empty. Ronnie was working at a hospital close by; the money for letting the room helped to keep Annie at the sanatorium, till she got well. Hilda would never forget the day she had shown Ronnie over Annie's room. It was, of course, the best in the house. Her parents were both out, and there was no one in but herself.

The house looked as nice as possible, because Mums, even if she was less educated than her daughter, kept it like that always; and Ronnie had been breathless and shy, but with manners that seemed in spite of his breathlessness to manage everything beautifully for both of them. He fell in love with the house. Hilda had given him tea, and they talked with a sudden startling intimacy emanating from Ronnie's intense and active charm. They talked and talked, and Ronnie had swiftly shown Hilda that she had the sort of intelligence he liked. At least he had thought so then.

Hilda knew she was not pretty, but she had a good figure, and her big dark eyes redeemed her face from positive plainness. Some people like red hair, when it is thick and glossy. Ronnie called it "a glorious Venetian!"

It was not really surprising that he slid into his easy love for her; took what he wanted (but for so short a time wanted); and then slowly tortured the life out of her.

Hilda knew all the things that could be said against Ronnie almost from the first; and she had very frequently, when roused, said them. Ronnie was too easy; he was vain. He was too sure of his own conquering charm; and when once it had conquered, too easily tired of the acquired object.

He was neither honest nor kind; but how enchanting he could be when he was pleased! How glittering were those easy manners and that ready tongue!

Hilda had forgiven and forgiven Ronnie's careless falsity. She had flamed up into furies, and sank back into sick despairs.

It was no use being angry with Ronnie; nor did he care how much he hurt her.

He was not ever going to be any different, any more loyal, any more kind!

He knew he had better manners, better chances in life than Hilda, and he meant to take them; however far apart they drew him from Hilda.

"Farewell! Thou are too dear for my possessing – and like enough thou knowest thy estimate." Shakespeare's young man friend must have been very like Hilda's; for Ronnie knew his estimate all right.

She too had discovered that she was "in sleep a king, on waking no such matter."

It was half her own fault too perhaps. She had wanted love too much; too much to hold back for a little thing like security. Well, she had got love, some of it at any rate – the sort of love, she told herself bitterly (finishing off Dr. Silla's letters, and hunting about for good stout envelopes that did not look too official), that people like Ronnie gave. If she had not wanted that kind of young man, she might have been safe with a sober little clerk; or a young tradesman with pimples, and a second-rate timid mind, the kind of mind people must have who leave school at fifteen, and have to earn a precarious two or three pounds a week for ever afterwards.

Hilda had wanted style and swagger; and for a time (a very short time) she had had it.

After all, she told herself, with the curious stubborn loyalty she still found at the bottom of her heart for Ronnie, he *had* done a good deal for her! He had cleared her pasty skin; and given colour to her cheeks and light to her eyes. He had freed her shackled mind, and set her heart rocking with rapture.

Why, she used to sing in her bath, and go to her work on wings, even if after their fierce quarrels she had wanted to throw herself under motor-buses!

She had had a year of this sweet and bitter loving

– before she had known that Ronnie was growing tired of her.

She wore herself out to serve and please him; at first he had liked being served and pleased by Hilda, but no man likes being served and pleased by the same woman for long. Hilda had found that though she must still serve Ronnie harder than ever, the pleasure had gone out of it.

Ronnie would have been unfaithful to her anyhow, Hilda reminded herself, unearthing the right envelopes at last, and slipping the letters with mechanical accuracy into their correct envelopes. He had never told her where he was going, or when he would be back, or with whom he spent their precious time. For he did not seem to realize that time *was* hers, as well as his.

He left her to garner up, as best she could, the fragments of his discarded hours, flinging the mere crumbs of his presence at her starving heart.

Hilda had taught herself to close her lips against the penury of Ronnie's long absences; but she had not taught herself to accept their being spent with Annie.

"He shan't do that!" she now said firmly, with a final sponge to the flaps of Dr. Silla's envelopes.

"Not to Annie as well as me! One in the family with a broken heart is quite enough!"

But how could she stop it? Could anything this woman, with *Nervenarzt* on her card, said help to stop it?

She might help Hilda from going mad; probably that would be what the lecture was about; but could she tell people how to prevent other people from *sending* them mad? "If I only knew how to stop them!" Hilda said for the thousandth time. "I'm not going to have a baby, so I can't palm that old stunt off on Ronnie – I dare say it wouldn't pull him up, if I did! Of course I could tell Annie he'd been my actual lover, but she'd be frightfully shocked. She's so strict one way (having been to that convent school) and yet so flighty, the other. That's the trouble; she leads men on and doesn't mean what she's leading them on to! At least I didn't do that with Ronnie! I paid for my fun. But if Annie was to get too upset either way – upset at my not being what she calls 'pure' – or upset at not getting Ronnie for herself – if she really wants him – it might make her lung break down again! I can't do *that* to Annie. If I tell Father and Mother, they'd only think I was – well – too awful for words! They're so old-fashioned, poor dears, they think girls *don't*, unless they *are* awful. I couldn't make them believe it was only Ronnie; and because it was the only way I could ever have him! Besides they'd be so miserable – they *like* Ronnie. Mums knows I'm not happy, but she doesn't know the reason. She thinks I just flirted with Ronnie and got through with it! I let her think it. I was so afraid of her finding out the truth. It's all very well saying old people know life better than young ones! I dare say they do, their own kind of life – the one they've *had* – but mine isn't *like* theirs! Mums never had a Ronnie. She can't know what that was like! Well, I suppose I must go home anyhow, Ronnie or no Ronnie – and I mustn't forget the tomatoes either! I'll be glad to get out of the house after supper again – even to go to a lecture. A good thing that foreign woman dropped in after all, for now I can pay for the wash this week!"

Hilda slipped both letters into her bag, tidied her desk for the next day, powdered her nose at the little looking-glass hanging on the wall, and glared at her strong but not unpleasing face. At least it was not unpleasing unless she glared.

Then she joined the rush hour. She did not forget the tomatoes, and while she was buying them she saw a bunch of particularly good radishes, and remembered how fond Annie was of them. These bunches looked crisper and fresher than usual, each single radish was as red as a cherry. "If I'm not going to let her have Ronnie," Hilda said to herself with a grim smile, "at least I may as well let her have radishes!"

Chapter 2

HILDA'S home was about as nice as a home can well be run on six pounds a week, with a little extra thrown in if the luck held.

Hilda's father only made two pounds a week now, because the business he worked for, as cashier, could not afford more. At one time he had been very well off, and earned the whole six, but – what with the slump, his age, and his not having the nerve to stand up for himself for fear of losing his job altogether – the firm had succeeded in beating him down to two.

Ronnie paid thirty shillings a week for half board and lodging. They made him extremely comfortable, and he stayed on after he had thrown over Hilda, because nobody knew he had thrown her over; and Hilda felt they had better have the money anyhow, and did not want wholly to lose the bitter-sweet company of Ronnie. Annie shared her sister's room since she had come back from Switzerland.

Ronnie had been most helpful about Annie. He had actually got her a job as a mannequin that might lead to good money later on. Annie's figure was lovely, but she had to stand for hours with heavy fur capes on her shoulders, so Hilda was not sure how long she would stick it, though at present – what with the fun of wearing lovely clothes all day, and being in love with Ronnie – Annie was as well as anything. Then there was Hilda's money, and they had all got to be dressed as well as fed, and have their holidays, cigarettes and cinemas.

Whether they got what they wanted, or approximately what they wanted, depended largely on Hilda.

Mrs. Fenchurch had never earned anything. She only worked from morning till night looking after the house, cooking, and making her family comfortable. She thought nothing of this, and had no grievances, except the kitchen sink, and the awkwardness of not having running water laid on in the bedrooms. It would, she said, have made all the difference. They all washed in the bathroom, but it was not quite the same thing, especially as Ronnie – though fortunately later than anyone else – always took more than his share of hot water and towels, and messed up everything. "After all, he pays for it," Mrs. Fenchurch would say consolingly. "Sweet as an angel when you give in to him – but you don't want to make him glum."

It sometimes seemed to Hilda that her mother – ignorant as she was – and devoted to Ronnie – was not, as the other three members of the family were, wholly taken in by him.

It was unfortunate for both Hilda and Annie that their parents were far less well educated than they were themselves.

Both girls loved their father and mother with shame, irritation, and an intense, though hitherto fruitless, desire to improve them. Their parents liked the wrong pictures, read the wrong books, and had a common way of talking.

Mr. Fenchurch was very much interested in politics, but they were, from his children's point of view, the wrong kind.

Mr. Fenchurch was, by nature and by choice, an under-dog, and it might have been supposed that he would have wished to support, or to see supported, other under-dogs; but he took exactly the opposite attitude. He wanted to be the *only* under-dog, and felt an intense resentment for any other. In his eyes the King, the Prime Minister, and any favourite general or admiral the popular Press upheld, were not only always right – but sacredly right; and the more mistaken any of these human beings were, the more sacred did their acts become. Mr. Fenchurch went still further; he clung passionately to all the "upper classes" and identified himself with their romances, their fortunes, and any of their blunders that came out in the Press. His children were out-and-out "Bolshies," as Mr. Fenchurch often told them, and even in Russia would have been executed or at least imprisoned for their insubordination. Only England was not Russia, and if you were not in the Government, it made no difference what you thought.

Mother took the position of the middle-party or buffer state.

She could not help thinking that all these dictators were a pity; and felt sorry for Abyssinia – Spain – and China. Still she did not think we ought to do anything about them. She remembered the War. As for these Russians, when we really wanted them in 1914, and thought they were in closed carriages with the blinds pulled down, all over England – they had turned out never to have left their own firesides, if at that time they had any! And later on, when they were thought of affectionately as "Steam Rollers" prepared to pass scatheless and repressive over entire German Army Corps – they had again acted against their characters, and, if anything, had been more rolled upon than rolling. So how were you to know?

Annie felt that it was not fair for some people to wear all that ermine and those pearls, and own their own Rolls Royces, while she had to hang on to a strap when she was tired, and buy everything at Woolworth's, or go without.

Hilda saw that it was no use even trying to reason with the rest of her family, for they thought what they liked, and were like what they thought.

Even before Ronnie came Hilda had been impatient with her family's mental processes, but on the whole she had controlled her intellectual irritation with her family, because she knew they all adored her, and believed her to be cleverer than any of them.

It was after Ronnie began to turn nasty, and use his own superior wits to show himself and them how far from clever Hilda really was, that Hilda became frankly savage with her family. Mainstays cannot be trifled with in the home circle; and Ronnie not only trifled with Hilda but he very cleverly dislodged the loyalty of her family, and taught them how to trifle with her too.

It was Ronnie's way of getting out of a disagreeable

situation, to turn the person he had failed into an object of reproach to those around her. By doing so he not only salved his own conscience, but had the sympathy of the others to fall back upon.

Hilda had read about those little fish that squirt ink over their enemies; and love did not blind her to the fact that spiritually Ronnie belonged to the same biological species.

When Hilda reached home, she saw immediately that there were flowers upon the table, and Ronnie's place laid. Dinner – for they had their chief meal at night – and only spent eightpence on their lunches – was the one meal Ronnie never took with them unless specially invited. He had a splendid breakfast in his bedroom, and rushed across from the hospital for a small lunch of a superior kind given him by "Mums," alone, who immensely enjoyed his single companionship – for Ronnie had a great gift with middle-aged women upon whom any of his comfort depended. He did not take tea, and was usually out in the evening.

Since he had broken with Hilda he had always been out in the evening, but Hilda knew that Annie had often been out with him.

"You've laid an extra place!" Hilda said in a severely accusing voice to her mother, handing her over the tomatoes.

"Splendid!" said Mums with that false heartiness that sometimes, but not often, disintegrates severity. "Such good ones – and radishes too! Well, I do call that a treat! I'll just make the salad, dear, while you wash. The others haven't come home yet. It's those buses – but what I say is, that if they're speeded up the way the papers want, how are you ever going to get inside them at all? Hop and cling – all in one piece, as it were – with people pushing in front of you, and trampling on you from behind? Inhuman is what I call it, and the tubes are worse, shutting their iron doors right on you – without even a man to shout at – ! Well yes – I *did* just lay that extra place in case Ronnie dropped in – he said something to Annie this morning, before she went out – after you'd gone – about Marlene Dietrich being on at the Royalty to-night – and they're both so mad about her! I'm like you – I've always liked Greta Garbo best. More style to her – if you know what I mean – Besides I like a woman that don't keep on pecking at you to notice her, and that Marlene – well, she seems to *expect* you to notice her – the same as if she were brought up on it!"

"They're all brought up on it," Hilda said wearily. "But Greta is the better artist! You're right there! If Ronnie drops in to dinner, I think he ought to pay a little more – he eats a lot of meat – and has the best room in the house anyway, and he always expects beer!"

"Well – I hardly like to ask him," Mrs. Fenchurch said thoughtfully, passing back into the kitchen. "He's so hard up, poor boy. Skinflints, his parents – as he once explained to me – though sometimes the clergy, if not archbishops and so on, seem worse off than anybody – and *have* to go to church on Sunday – so you see their clothes *must* be what they ought! A great mercy clothes are so much cheaper nowadays, except wool – you can't get good woollen things cheap – say what you like. That's the reason I knit all yours and Annie's pullovers!"

Hilda was half-way up the stairs before her mother got to the pullovers. So she only grunted by way of an answer.

When Hilda had washed and slipped on a jade-green dress – a dress that Ronnie had once loved her in (she had to go on wearing it, whatever she felt like, for fashions change so quickly, and she had spent more on it than she could afford, to please Ronnie), Hilda saw Annie coming in at the front door. Annie looked so radiant that wings might have been attached to her slim sloping shoulders.

She was dazzlingly fair, with cornflower-blue eyes,

and hair with a slightly reddish tinge – a dangerously clear skin over which the sweetest shell-pink colour spread or receded, as her feelings demanded.

Hilda loved Annie's little face – just too small for films, but with the sweetest rosebud mouth and tip-tilted nose.

Annie was very careful of her looks – almost as careful as Hilda wanted her to be. She had not good eyebrows, so she had to touch them up; and Hilda had advised her to slant them a little. "You look like a Leonardo, Annie," Hilda told her with pride, "and all his women's lips and eyes, and eyebrows and things, lift just a little!" She had not scolded Annie for thinking Leonardo's must be a beauty shop off Bond Street; and had even told her quite patiently who he really was, so that Ronnie should not laugh at her for not knowing.

Hilda knew just how Annie was feeling now, in that pretty striped frock they had given her at her shop after the sales were over – Annie felt like a queen. And for a moment Hilda felt like a queen too; then she remembered that she was a queen dethroned.

She did not hate her rival, but she hated the hand that raised Annie to so precarious a throne. She heard her father's voice, "Mother, you'd hardly believe what those Reds are after in Spain. I picked up the *Stand-*

ard in the tube, – a disgraceful waste to leave a fresh paper behind like that, – but for once I got it before one of those workmen that could probably afford an evening paper every night of his life if he liked, sticking at nothing and earning two hundred a year! Not that most workingmen choose the *Standard* to read, but I must say I agree with the fellow that writes these articles – we ought to back Franco more – although you can see for yourself, the Government's doing what it can – "

"Yes, dear, yes!" Mother's voice came soothingly from the kitchen – a little absorbed in dishing up. "Anything to stop all the trouble they must be having, poor things – though I'd have taken one of those Basque children myself, if they'd been allowed to come singly, and Ronnie hadn't been using the spare room. It's the bombs I mind – whatever they call themselves! I think I'll bring the steak in now, it's done to a turn, and Ronnie hates it overdone, even if he's late! I hope you won't mind having bread-and-butter pudding, Annie. I've put in those large kitchen raisins you like so much, though the time it takes stoning them! And the crust's beautiful, if I say it myself – I know you don't like cooked-up things, but you've got to use what's in the house sometimes, or where would we all be?"

Annie said in a low dreamy voice: "Why should I mind, Mums? I'm not hungry, anyhow – and oh, there's radishes with the salad – how nice – you won't mind if I eat salad instead of pudding, will you?"

Mums sighed and murmured, "I'd better have done those banana fritters after all!"

Hilda helped her mother carry in the trays. She was setting down the meat and vegetables when Ronnie came in, so that nobody noticed her lack of greeting.

"If *he'd* been a plate I was holding, I'd have let it crash!" Hilda said to herself.

Ronnie's eyes met hers. He gave Hilda a long, steady, poisonous look – the look of a man who knows his power over a beaten cur, and enjoys it; but he had made a mistake, for Hilda was not beaten. She had been both wronged and heartbroken, but nothing in her had been beaten. Something strong in her remained by which she could build herself up again. She did not yet know how, but she knew that she still had this power. They sat down at table all a little hungry and tired, only Annie and Ronnie were gay as well as tired. Before them stretched a world all to themselves, through lighted, laughing streets, wild with excitement and spectacular dreams.

Annie's joy was greater than Ronnie's, because she

did not have to do anything about it. Her happy, loving heart was not playing a game or trying to get control of anything.

Annie was very easily made happy, but she never tried to do anything about it. She just stood there — tall and slender, with her eyes very wide open, and her gentle, smiling lips a little apart; and if you were anxious to serve her she took the service, with her slow, beaming smile, and if you disappointed her, she was just as gentle, and waited for something or somebody else to turn up who would not disappoint her. She had never had to wait very long; and Hilda had usually been the one who saw that Annie got what she wanted.

After dinner was over, Ronnie drew out a cigarette and said with his charming smile, "Isn't Hilda going to give us a cup of her famous coffee for a treat?" He liked to say these things in public, to see what Hilda would do — usually she put herself in the wrong, by a refusal so sharp that one of her parents had to rebuke her; but to-night she got up without a word, and went into the kitchen to make Ronnie his coffee. It was not that she felt less angry — on the contrary she was more angry still; but the difference was that she knew now that she was going to do something with her anger, whereas until now it had felt useless.

"Now, I suppose," she said to herself, "if there were arsenic handy, and I knew how to use it – as the people in books always seem to do, on the spur of the moment, though if they're not chemists or doctors, one would think they wouldn't know how – I'd put it in Ronnie's cup, and get everything washed up and put away, before it had started working! The trouble is, you mustn't have *bought* the poison – that's how you get found out! Still if I knew how to do it – I'd stand a pretty good chance, because, thank God, I've held my tongue and no one knows how I hate him!"

They drank the coffee after that, and Ronnie thanked Hilda for it with double-edged words. Then they went out – Ronnie and Annie together – too happy for laughter.

Mr. Fenchurch took out his pipe and unfolded the fortunately gleaned *Standard*. "Mother," he said, "as soon as you've finished washing up I've got an article on air raids to read to you. It's time we did something about ordering gas-masks, especially if the Government's going to pay for them!"

"Yes, dear," his wife answered with cheerful alacrity, "I'd be glad to do a little darning – while you read aloud to me; but I hope we shan't have to wear anything suffocating over our faces – and babies, you know, can't! I should think it would be better for everybody if gas weren't used, except in ovens, where it rightly belongs! Though, as I dare say you've seen, they've actually raised the price again – I suppose because they want more of it to kill the others with, when they begin. It's very good of you to help me, Hilda dear, but don't you want to go out?"

"Yes," said Hilda, "I am going out, to a lecture, by a foreigner – on people's minds – but I'll dry the dinner things first for you – it goes quicker with two."

"There's another murder case," Mr. Fenchurch went on, raising his voice to meet the running of the taps, and getting the better of them, by an effort. "One of those man-and-girl things – tore off her clothes and stamped all over her! I don't see what we're coming to, Mary – I don't really – in my young days murders were just plain murders, not these 'cream passional,' as the French call them. I believe we picked them up from the French during the War, and that's the reason the Government want to make friends with Germany instead now. You can't blame them!"

"Nonsense, Father!" Hilda said sharply. "Look at that German pervert – killed thirty-nine women, and how? The French aren't any worse than we are, if as bad – besides there are more horrible crimes than murder, anyhow — these people that go off the rails and kill their friends, you don't know what they've had to put up with first!"

"That's right," Mother said quickly. "What we see in the paper, that's just the wind-up, as it were! Still you know, Hilda, I've never thought these cold-blooded *planned* murders were excusable! Like or dislike, we've got to put up with each other — or else we won't get put up with, ourselves — that's how I look at it!"

Hilda went on wiping the dinner things. She was conscious that her mother had spoken quickly to defend what would be, to her, indefensible; and that she had done it because, beyond reason and knowledge, she had sensed that her child spoke out of a cruel pain. All her family were dear to Mrs. Fenchurch. Her husband was the man of her choice, and after twenty-five years' ups and downs, she would still have chosen him. He was dismal but kind; and at a pinch could be stubbornly heroic. Annie, she had had great trouble in rearing, and there was nothing her mother would not have sacrificed for Annie then or now; but Hilda was different. Mrs. Fenchurch admired Hilda. She knew her for what she was — a strong, capable girl, willing to do her full share of everything that had to be done, and strictly loyal to the last drop of her blood – quick-tempered and snappish certainly – and would have her own way wherever it led – but you could not want a better daughter, or one that you could be more certain would under no circumstances whatever let you down.

"Hilda," she said in a low voice, so that her husband could not overhear and chip in with something that might upset the girl, "Hilda, your holiday hasn't done you any good! You've gone all purple under your eyes, just as if you'd never gone away at all! You work too hard, that's what it is, and this lecture now – on the mind – well, I ask you – is that a nice cheerful subject after a long day's work? And by a foreigner too – what can you expect? It seems to me that what you *really* want is to get things *out* of your mind – not into it! Those Marx brothers your father and I saw last Saturday night when you wouldn't go – well, you couldn't keep anything on your mind – not for a minute – looking at them!"

Hilda refused to smile, or even to answer her mother's remarks, but she felt vaguely gratified by her concern.

She knew it made no difference whether she confided in her mother or not – or how little her mother actually knew of what went on behind the mask of Hilda's face, since she was well aware that her mother knew unerringly what was in her daughter's heart. That link between them had never been broken.

"Still she doesn't know I want to *kill* Ronnie," Hilda told herself defensively. "She isn't even sure — though she may suspect — that what's the matter with me *is* Ronnie — but she knows well enough that I'm down and out! and she's the only person in the world that I don't *mind* knowing it!" Aloud she said, rather grumpily, "It won't be a bad lecture, and I hate being made to laugh! Don't sit up for me, either of you — I have my key!" She did not kiss either of her parents or say good night, because she saw that her father expected it.

Chapter 3

DOWNSTAIRS Hilda heard the monotonous drone of her father's voice reading out loud to her mother any particular atrocity that struck his fancy out of the evening paper; since Mrs. Fenchurch had no choice in the matter, she often deflected her mind towards her own particular problems, but she could be counted on to remain in the same room while Mr. Fenchurch's voice went on.

Even if her parents heard Hilda moving about overhead in Ronnie's sacred precincts, they wouldn't be surprised, for hadn't Hilda a right to help her mother by tidying them up, before she set out for her lecture?

Ronnie loved order; but although he liked the perfected article, he had never been known to take any steps to produce it. On the contrary, as he was always in a hurry to be going on somewhere else, Ronnie made a habit of flinging all his clothes on the floor in a heap, as he got out of them.

He slopped his wash-stand, and left it slopped; he expected his brush and comb to be cleared of all possible hairs without his attempting to remove them; while taking it as a matter of course that his boots should be cleaned, he failed to put them outside the door; and in many other ways he demonstrated how precious he was to an attentive world – and how much upkeep this preciousness naturally entailed.

Once or twice, while he was still in love with Hilda, Ronnie, referring to the exquisite neatness and freshness with which his room was kept, spoke of "Hilda's special magic," but even Hilda knew – once his love had cooled – how silly it was to go on tidying his room.

She had had the sense to let everything else go. She no longer greeted Ronnie's entrances or hovered over his exits. He could – delicate as he was and always catching colds he referred to as "mine" – go out in any weather now without a muffler.

But his room was still kept as gay and light as a sweet pea, with all his well-chosen ties hanging uncreased on separate pegs; his handkerchiefs washed and ironed by Hilda on her Saturdays, without a hint of starch; and every shoe keeping its symmetry intact, by the help of its appropriate tree.

Hilda guessed that Ronnie did not think the more of her for these ministrations; nor the less of himself for continuing to accept them.

But there was in Hilda a strange craving that she was quite unable to justify, to overwhelm Ronnie with secret generosities.

She still wanted him to have all the creature comforts of a mate – without fulfilling any of a mate's obligations.

Ronnie was her first lover, perhaps in the real sense of the word he would be her only one, since after a first lover, all others are but imitations of a bygone rapture.

There may have been no sense in smoothing out his trousers upon a trouser-press he had airily hinted she might give him as a Christmas present; but once they were correctly disposed of, and his coat straightened out upon a padded hanger, Hilda's heart felt undeniably lighter.

While he was still under her roof, nothing could break down her knowledge of Ronnie's tastes, or quench her will to gratify them.

In these matters Annie was no rival, for Annie

never even envisaged attentions *for* lovers, only attentions *from* them.

Suddenly, a letter dropped from Ronnie's still swinging pocket onto the floor; it was addressed, in Ronnie's own delicate flowing handwriting, to a middle-aged woman whom Ronnie despised and from whom he often borrowed. Hilda knew all about her. She was a friend and contemporary of Ronnie's mother; and Ronnie had swooped upon her, with all his desperate charms spread out like a hawk's talons, to catch in their grip her elderly vanity. She had been a great beauty in her youth, and something of it still remained. His "Hag Beauty," as Ronnie styled her, omitting to mention that the phrase was first Arnold Bennett's, had afforded him a good deal of entertainment, but an entertainment which Hilda had never been able to share.

She had often wondered what Ronnie's real attitude to the woman herself was. Now she could find out. Hilda knew that there was nothing whatever to be said for reading a letter not addressed to oneself.

But only those who have all the letters they want; no interest whatever in the writer; or so much self-respect that it does not occur to them to do in private what they would shrink from in public, are wholly beyond the reach of this particular temptation.

Hilda picked the letter up from the floor, sat down on the edge of the bed, and read it.

Dearest Star [Ronnie began, although the lady's name was Alice],

What a wonderful thing it is to have a mind to write to! If you only knew what I have to suffer from these half-baked chits one seems at my age fated to go about with! Thank God Hilda has at last accepted the situation! I did what you advised and told her – man to man – that the whole thing was off. I hated doing it of course, and there were the usual reactions – tears; threats; recriminations. If only girls had learned to practise the exquisite tact and restraint of older women. A woman like yourself for instance – to whom love is both more and less than a physical tie, never makes a man feel like a cad when his side of it has to be withdrawn. Fortunately you were right as usual, Hilda carried out none of her threats; and finding that tears neither moved me, nor suited her, soon mopped them up. I'm still under the same roof, which may surprise you a little, but as a man of what I suppose one still has to call honour – I had to try to preserve what little self-respect the poor girl lets herself keep. Rushing off on the spur of the moment looked too much of an open slight to her. Besides, as you know, I happen to be the chief prop of the family's finances, and in their simple way they have all been terribly nice to me.

Don't worry about the little sister. She's as pretty as a speedwell in a country lane, and just about as common! Well, good-bye! Do you mind if I just leave it open about the week-end and blow in if I can escape the clutches of the Cormorant?

Your devoted RONNIE.

The "Cormorant" was the playful name Ronnie gave to his mother.

Hilda folded the letter carefully, and, licking down the flap of the envelope, placed it on the dressing-table where Ronnie would think he had left it, when he came in.

She had a passing impulse to share it with Annie, nor was it a moral scruple, or even the fact of having to give herself away, that restrained her. Hilda simply wasn't quite sure enough of Annie.

She mightn't *be* moved to give up Ronnie. Annie was a wolf for compliments and to be called as "pretty as a speedwell" could be taken as a compliment, if you ignored the sting of the "common."

Annie might not accept this phrase with Hilda's vulnerability; and she might think the whole letter – "half-baked chits" and all – a mere ruse on Ronnie's part to keep an old cat quiet.

Annie herself was a bit of a twister, and her morality often changed colour against the stronger colour schemes of her wishes.

Hilda sat with the letter in her lap, staring at the open door of the wardrobe, where Ronnie's three well-brushed suits still stirred a little, after her tidying.

There seemed, she thought, so many ways to end love, each one cheaper and shabbier than the last.

Hilda had once watched, in impotent fury, half-a-dozen yokels burn up a blind worm with a box of matches. She had stamped and shrieked and battled with her baby hands, for she was only four years old at the time, but she hadn't been able to save the worm; and she had never forgotten how long it took before it ceased to writhe.

She thought of it again now, and thinking of it made her feel sick.

"I shan't tear the letter up," Hilda said to herself drearily. "What's the use? He'll only write her another – he's full of letters like that! She'll just have to shift for herself – when she finds out – as I've done. '*Spillfeathers, Baresfrere, Near Dover*' – must be close to Auntie's. I might look it up one of these days, if Ronnie isn't there. Probably he'll go off to some other friends after all – and pretend they're his mother! It's odd how often he doesn't get found out! I wonder if the poor old thing knew what he really thought of her – would she go on caring for him?"

Hilda's thoughts hovered with a strange agony of concentration over the "Hag Beauty," who to-morrow would be so pleased to read Ronnie's lying letter.

"Perhaps," Hilda said to herself, "a physical love, as he calls it, is worse than what she feels! She's got a husband and a garden full of roses." . . . "Roses as wild as she'd like to be herself, if she hadn't skipped the age for it," Ronnie had once wittily remarked. Would that get her if she knew he'd said it? Would it have got Hilda? "But I'm different," Hilda told herself fiercely. "I've been his mistress for a year! So I've got all mixed up. I want him – the way one would want a part of oneself if it had been cut off! One just doesn't seem able to walk about without it! And yet wouldn't it hurt more still if I'd never been Ronnie's – but had thought how awfully he had admired and respected me – and then found out that he'd been laughing at me all the time? That woman has never had anything real at all!

"What a born liar Ronnie is! I've never cried before him! He never stood up to me and told me it was over – it just petered out! I've never threatened him! It's true I've spoken pretty sharply to him and told him what I've thought of him. He has *that* to go on with! My God! He shan't get away with that 'speedwell' nastiness! Annie is common, is she? I'd like to wring his neck for that!"

Hilda still sat, on the edge of the bed, nor had she once moved; but now her stillness had a more ominous quality, as if the secret of movement had been frozen out of her. "Well, why don't you kill him then?" a voice within her cried loudly.

This voice wasn't like the idea she'd had in the kitchen about putting arsenic into Ronnie's coffee – that had simply blown into her mind and blown out again, like reading the caption of a film; you saw it in a flash, knew what it meant, and the next moment it was gone. But this thought did not come from without; it had welled up out of some strange depths in her; and though it was shortly to sink back again, it did not go away.

"People do kill their lovers," Hilda told herself defensively, "and though some of them get found out, I expect a lot don't! Look at all the books about it, and the real things in the papers! You've got to keep your head of course, after you've done it, and go on living as usual. Well, thank God I've got an office to myself anyhow, even if I haven't got a bedroom!"

Hilda got up stiffly. She didn't put on a hat; but she produced a powder-puff, and, standing in front of Ronnie's looking-glass, she powdered her face and was careful to blow all the powder off the dressing-table afterwards; because Ronnie hated to see a grain of it about, in spite of saying that more men gave up girls for shiny noses than for any other lapse in either their morals or their manners.

Hilda drew her comb cautiously through the thick mop of her red-brown hair; and wished that she had a shorter upper lip. Annie had; and it made her look lovely when she smiled.

Then Hilda ran downstairs rather noisily and banged the front door after her, so that her parents should know that she had gone to the lecture after all. She found herself strolling through the Fulham High Street with an odd detached feeling, as if she were no longer taking up any room on the pavement. She had ceased to be an ordinary person hurrying home to a late supper, carrying with her a sort of invisible net full of the day's catch. Her mind was empty of all its familiar activities.

"Murder"! That was a word, when once it came running through your mind, that drove out every other thought.

There was something urgent about it, like the bell of a fire engine, forcing its way through traffic.

Even if people were having the jitters over Nazis and Bolshies; even if Almería was crying to the pitiless skies in vain; or thousands of Chinese swept away by their Yellow River — one murder in a London slum, would take their place on all the placards.

"Murder of a Medical Student," for instance, how that would stare out at people from every street corner, or outside each stationer's shop; and how different, how paralyzingly different it would look if Hilda herself knew more about it than all the newspapers!

Hilda had felt impotent, before, whenever she thought of Ronnie; and now she felt almost too powerful, because she saw that she could stop there being any more Ronnie.

Not arsenic, even if she could get hold of it; and not strychnine, because that gave you convulsions, and she could not bear to think of anyone writhing like that poor blind worm; but nobody could mind some nice safe narcotic!

The only trouble about it, as a method for murder, was that the victim might not be left undisturbed long enough to die of it. Still it could be thought out. If it happened when Mums and Dad were on their annual visit to the Catesbys at Birmingham, for instance? Ronnie had to stay on late in London this year on account of his examinations. Annie slept like a pig — and after the milkman had called, there wouldn't be anyone coming to the house till the girls got back from work.

If Ronnie got his narcotic in sufficient quantities over night, he would be pretty sure to die of it. But it wasn't going to be easy to get enough down him without its tasting queer.

"I should have to find out all kinds of things," Hilda told herself doubtfully, for by now she was beginning to suffer a sort of reaction. The first fury of her impulse roused by Ronnie's letter had begun to die down.

"More about the tastes of poisons, for instance, and what quantities. A pity I can't ask the foreign lady, because she's leaving England so soon."

Hilda had a thorough mind, and although the impulse had already become a little unreal to her, she thought the rest of the story carefully out. "I could leave the bottle by his bedside, with the glass and everything, and get his own fingerprints on them first by some trick. He'd look as if he'd taken an overdose by mistake – as some people do." The fact that some people take overdoses of narcotics by mistake suddenly seemed to Hilda a pleasing trait. But by now she had arrived at the Conway Hall, and had to show Dr. Silla's card at the door. She was late, and was allowed in, with a mere glance at it.

There was a pretty good audience as lecture audiences go, and Hilda felt pleased. She wanted the foreign lady's lecture to be a success; and for the moment, looking round at the interested unknown faces, she thought no more of Ronnie.

Chapter 4

HILDA knew that she would have enjoyed the lecture had she been able to concentrate upon it.

The lecturer had a good manner. She stood on the centre of the platform, and faced her audience with a friendly steadiness.

There they were – she seemed to say – a nice set of reasonably intelligent people – or else they would not be there, prepared to share with her the subject of the evening. She had prepared this subject thoroughly, and therefore could give them a reliable account of it.

Dr. Elena Silla spoke slowly and clearly; and evidently what she said was interesting as well as new to her audience, for they followed every point, and often broke into applause or laughter.

But Hilda could follow nothing but the hard pelting of her bitter thoughts, and yet a curious thing happened to Hilda. Although she could not listen to the lecturer's words, she felt invaded by a quality of the lecturer herself, a quality that made her earlier thoughts that evening, – Ronnie's letter, the "Hag Beauty's" feelings, – even Annie's danger, – seem less vivid to her.

"Perhaps," Hilda thought, with a great wave of relief, "perhaps I needn't murder Ronnie after all!"

It was not so simple to hate Ronnie, when she had trained herself to love every hair of his head – that was the worst of loving; it included everything – you could not say: "This human being has such and such repulsive qualities; he has done such and such vicious actions; he has said such and such cruel words – therefore I will hate him!" Suppose all these things were true, they weren't the *whole* of the person you loved!

Ronnie had given Hilda heaven as well as hell. He had told her exquisite things about herself, he had lifted her above the pinch and drudgery of time. He had enjoyed her; and by enjoying her, he had enriched her capacity for giving enjoyment.

Hilda had always wanted to give, but she had been frightened and mistrustful of the value of her gifts.

She was doubtful of her own merits, as a human being, certain of the poverty of her attractions – contemptuous of being a girl at all. Ronnie had brushed aside all these doubts and impediments.

He had made a drama for her in which she could play an overwhelmingly important part; and, just as she was learning to play it really well, he had pushed her off the stage – out into the empty world again. When she had tried to get back, he had made her feel lower than a street girl.

"If that's what you wanted," he once told her when, desperate for his familiar kindness, she had gone one night to his room, "you ought to have learned your job – any street girl knows it better!"

That had been enough to make Hilda's withdrawal final; and she *had* withdrawn herself; but even this complete severing of the physical tie between them had not enabled her to keep Ronnie's image at bay.

There it always was, dancing before her eyes, like a mirage before the eyes of a thirsty traveller: the shape of his head – the charming way his rather colourless light eyes flickered over her – his sudden smile that sweetened the discontented lines of his long face into unexpected beauty! She never got Ronnie's least careless gesture out of her head, nor the touch of his thin, well-kept hands, nor the quick patter of his speech, coming in little gusts and rushes as if he were nervous – which he never was; or impulsive – which he was still less.

Hilda herself had rather a good mind, nourished on books, but only used to the dry bread of speech – the kind of slangy, pointless communications without choice or care that passed for conversation in her home circle. Suddenly to hear – and to share – the fruits of the mind, pressed into neat, quick turns of speech, was like watching a champion tennis player at the nets, after seeing children play pat-ball.

Hilda had listened to Ronnie's talk, breathless with delight. He said things she did not think people ought to say – or *could* say even if they ought; and out of her own awkward hesitating mind, Hilda had learned to draw happy turns of speech to meet his.

She had let thought out – and this unchained watchdog had gambolled about with such delight, in the free air of intimacy, that Hilda felt it cruelly hard to have to lock him up again.

Hilda had hoped that Ronnie would be satisfied, as indeed he was for a time, with his triumphant empire over her ripening mind. Unfortunately Hilda's mind went on ripening with a speed, and in a direction, that by no means always suited Ronnie. Ronnie thought that people's minds should be used first to get what one wanted when other means failed — these were the mind's *invisible* processes and should not be drawn attention to — and second to amuse oneself when other more expensive diversions were unobtainable. These were the mind's *visible* processes, and should be polished up with sufficient care. Hilda seemed to think that once thought was free, it was a kind of touchstone that ought to be used, with inconvenient logic, upon everything. Nor did she deal with any discrimination between what should be visible or invisible processes — out came all her thoughts helter-skelter, like a rock stream bounding down upon Ronnie, from a mountain-side.

Was it any wonder that he preferred the less exciting and infinitely safer society of Annie? Besides, Annie was not only more lovely — she was more difficult; and she was new.

Ronnie had told Hilda that not to give when you loved was ungenerous — and then he had despised her for giving. What, she asked herself, would he tell Annie; and how would little Annie — defenceless and passive by nature — be able to resist Ronnie's inspired urgency?

Ronnie did not frighten or hurry his prey; he waited, until the heart he played with grew more ardent than his own.

This lecturer said, among other things, that if you knew why people acted as they did, and why you yourself acted as you did, you could often avoid catastrophe in human relationships.

What did she mean by that? "How could I," Hilda asked herself, "have protected myself against Ronnie? However well I knew his reasons for doing things? I know them all now – and yet I don't feel particularly protected!"

The trouble was – words or no words – Hilda was past protection. Ronnie was in her blood! The point was, now, how could she prevent his getting into Annie's? He ran in Hilda's veins like a slow poison.

Like poison – that was the second time this evening Hilda had found herself thinking of the word "poison." There it was again – that word poison. Firmer and firmer embedded in her mind, each time she came upon it – and she seemed to come upon it so often too! It hardly seemed to have anything to do with herself now; but had become a part of her.

Good heavens – she had quite forgotten to post her client's two letters! She had them in her bag still. Fortunately there would be time on her way home, to catch the midnight post. It only showed what this business about Ronnie was doing with her wits!

Mums was right, her holiday had not done her

any good. How could it? Ronnie had taken her to Brighton to start with, for a week-end. It had rained all the time, and Ronnie had made Hilda responsible for the rain – and for the horrid cheating landlady who could not cook, and would not believe they were married. Perhaps, this last time, Ronnie had not taken his usual trouble to get the landlady to believe it.

It *was* the last time; and Hilda spent the rest of her holiday with her aunt near Dover, getting over Ronnie.

The aunt was a schoolteacher, whom Hilda had always adored, – she had done a great deal to develop and encourage her favourite niece's mind, – and now, to her horror, Hilda discovered that her aunt was "bourgeois"! "Common" was really what Hilda meant by "bourgeois," because Ronnie had taught her that "bourgeois" was the proper word for "common." It meant the same thing and sounded less snobbish.

"Sticky – bogus – bourgeois," with this happy trinity of disparagement, Ronnie had taught Hilda you could condemn and judge – without the danger of being considered superior; and yet if you used such words properly, you *were* superior!

Hilda caught the lecturer saying that people should not be judged by words or even thoughts – solely by their acts, and the life-plan on which these acts would be found to be based; even then they should not be judged in a moral way – but merely understood.

"Criminal negligence," for instance, was a very right term – for if you really cared for other people's safety you would never be negligent to the point of endangering it. You, in other words, *wanted* to be negligent before you became criminal; and you *became* criminal because you wanted to be negligent. It was the same piece of elastic, only you stretched it further. What a very curious idea, Hilda thought, before her mind fluffed off again to Ronnie.

Something familiar about the looks of the lecturer brought Hilda's mind back again, partly the way she stood there – straight and solid as a tower – and something in her expressive eyes that changed with her thoughts but were always clear – so that her sincerity was mirrored in them without ripple or blur. What was it Ronnie had once said to Hilda? They were not his own words – it was what a dead poet had said of a woman he must really have loved: "You are so true; you make dreams true; and fables histories."

Ronnie had quoted this to Hilda as a compliment, long ago, at a time when he had liked Hilda to be true.

It suddenly struck her now that perhaps the lecturer really looked a little like herself – only a good deal *more* true. More *real*, was what Hilda perhaps meant, and a great deal less broken-up and distracted. Physically the lecturer's build was the same, but she was not as tall as Hilda, and her hair was straighter, although exactly the same shade; her features, too, were not unlike Hilda's – a little heavy, but capable of lighting up. If Hilda had been dressed in black, with a hat on, people might well have mistaken her for this Dr. Silla. What a very curious idea, Hilda thought.

"So that really, if I went to the Laboratory to-morrow – I mean if I hadn't posted the letter – and they still expected Dr. Silla, they'd think I was her! Dr. Silla said she hadn't met any of the Laboratory people, so that even if one of them were here to-night at the lecture, they might be fooled! They keep all kinds of things in Laboratories. I know – because Ronnie told me: tubes with germs of diseases in them – as well as poisons. Curious diseases that people don't have over here! If I went – if I pretended I was Dr. Silla – I might take a poison or something bad in a tube away with me, and no one would ever find out! How could they – Dr. Silla would be in her own country, and not have done it anyway – and I shouldn't exist for them! Of course, it's only an idea.

Funny that to-night in the kitchen I was thinking about poison, and how difficult it would be not to trace how one got it – and now – there's this idea! But, of course, I shan't do it! Besides, if I can get Annie to give up Ronnie, it's all right – I don't want to hurt Ronnie, just in order to hurt him – only to save Annie! I'll try *first* – I'll try to-night – but perhaps I'd better not post that letter! If it's all right, and Annie gives Ronnie up, I can take the letter to the Laboratory on my way to work to-morrow, so that it would get there in time just the same. It isn't far! But if Annie won't . . . ? Still, I'm sure she will! After all, she's only known Ronnie a few weeks – and she's done what I've told her all her life! If I went to that laboratory to-morrow, and they *did* find out it wasn't Dr. Silla – I should just say it was a lark! After all, my life is as dull as hell. Why shouldn't I do a bit of play-acting – the same as anyone else? I was always the best of them at the Dramatic Club. I mustn't start talking like Mums – Ronnie doesn't like it. It's bourgeois!" Funny, Hilda felt, still caring what Ronnie liked, when she was planning to kill him! She had better begin to listen to the lecturer again, or else she would not know what psychiatrists – or whatever they called themselves – talked like! Not that it really mattered, as of course Annie *would* give in – and Hilda would not have to go to the Laboratory.

The lecture stopped soon after that – not dramatically, but as if the lecturer had said all she knew and was not going to say one word more than she knew.

It gave you a queer settled feeling, as if what she had said *must* be true.

There was a good deal of applause, and after Dr. Silla had bowed twice, – the first time gravely, the second time with a little friendly smile, – she caught sight of Hilda standing near the platform on her way out, and looked straight at her.

The look went travelling on inside Hilda's mind, just like the reverberation of a bell in a noiseless place. She could not get rid of it for quite a long time afterwards.

It was such a nice look! As if something solid had been established between them, the sort of natural tie that binds one reliable person to another. It was the same feeling Hilda had when she and Mums were doing a bit of work together. When you were working with Dad or Annie – or worse still with Ronnie – they would put it down long before they had done their bit. They would often have a perfectly good reason for putting it down, but anyhow you could be pretty sure that you would have to finish it as well as your own – if it was to be done at all! But with Mums you knew she would go on – as you would go on – until the job was finished.

This look the lecturer gave Hilda, accompanied by a little nod, was quite unquestioning and confident. It seemed to say, "I know you've done what you undertook to do, my letters *are* posted – and I feel as happy about it as if I'd posted them myself."

And they had not *been* posted! There they lay, with the weight of stones, in Hilda's bag.

It was a bitterly uncomfortable moment, and Hilda hung her head. She felt the discomfort pierce through and through her, but her intention remained the same. She would not post the second letter on her way home.

She shuffled out of the hall, with her head lowered, wishing she were dead.

Curiously enough, although she wished she were dead, the thought of suicide had never seriously occurred to Hilda, nor did it occur to her now. She was a bread-winner, important to her family, and a fighter, important to herself. She did not think Ronnie was of any such importance.

Chapter 5

THE FENCHURCHES lived in Rostrevor Road, somewhere to the north of Edith Grove.

It was not a prosperous neighbourhood, but the street itself was definitely respectable. Only people who could afford – or if not afford, could pay – fifty pounds a year rent lived in it.

Drunken, vicious or noisy people went elsewhere. You could, of course, hear the buses thundering by; nightly aeroplanes; factory whistles, and at least two neighbours' radios; but there was no publichouse at the corner, nor did the street's own children play in the gutter. Nothing audible of a sinister nature took place there. People died sometimes in Rostrevor Road, but not oftener than anywhere else; and they were born rather less often. Not that its inhabitants had any prejudice against adding to the human race, if such additions were sufficiently propped-up by marriage lines and wedding rings; but respectable people, who pay rents that are too high for them, do not have more children than they can help.

When Hilda went to bed, after the lecture on psychology, Rostrevor Road seemed quieter than usual. Hilda could hear the clock in the kitchen ticking, and infrequent footsteps sounded as if they were coming through the walls.

There was plenty of time to rehearse what Hilda meant to say to Annie, for Annie was unlikely to come back with Ronnie much before twelve.

After the cinema, Ronnie would probably take Annie to a café club, a little rakish – where there was dancing, and people knew each other by sight – but nothing to upset the police.

Ronnie had often taken Hilda to this club; so she knew all its ways.

A quick mind like Hilda's rehearses scenes in lightning flashes; and if there is only one scene to rehearse, the effort becomes monotonous. There was almost too much time before Annie and Ronnie came back.

Hilda varied the scene, of course, because she had

the sense to realize that it was not altogether *her* scene: It depended largely upon Annie's mood. One cannot ensure another person's reactions, however carefully one leads up to them.

Fortunately there was no antagonism between the two sisters. Their relationship had always been serene and confident. Annie had always wanted Hilda's protection and her practical services; Hilda had always wished to give Annie these practical services, and to protect her.

Each had wholly different qualities, and each admired the other's, and felt undisturbed by them, in the practice of her own.

Nor were they jealous of their parents' affection. Annie knew that her father loved her better than he loved Hilda, but that he respected Hilda more; whereas Mrs. Fenchurch loved her first-born more than Annie, but was prepared to give way more to her youngest on account of Annie's greater delicacy. Annie did not want to be respected, if it meant giving up being catered for, and Hilda did not want to be catered for, if it meant giving up being respected.

This involved an unusually peaceful and pleasant family life, with only a few rows every now and then, because Hilda was a little too domineering, and Annie a little too spoilt. When they had rows, Mr. Fenchurch supported Annie, but gave in to Hilda if she frightened him; and Mrs. Fenchurch usually supported Hilda, but sometimes swerved to Annie's side, if Annie seemed too much upset.

When Mrs. Fenchurch and Hilda stood up to each other, fur flew; but this seldom happened. When it did, if the point at issue was a practical one Mrs. Fenchurch usually came off best.

"Well, that's enough now, Hilda!" she would end by saying. "Take it or leave it!" And Hilda, having said she was going to leave it, after a decent interval – sufficient to save her face – usually took it. However, if the question were intellectual, the process would be reversed. Mrs. Fenchurch would conclude by giving in to Hilda, though not without referring to the doubtful end of young people. Still, while almost venerating her eldest daughter's superior knowledge, and often willing to give way to it, Mrs. Fenchurch thought that her own common sense had had a longer run for its money.

Sometimes the knowledge that her mother disagreed with her had been a great help to Hilda. Unfortunately she could not ask her mother now whether she agreed with her or not; and when the thought of how little her mother *could* agree with murder came into Hilda's mind, she hastily brushed it aside.

Hilda had posted the letter to Dr. Silla's friend, but the letter to the Laboratory was still in her bag. After she had rehearsed her scene with Annie so often that she forgot what she was going to say and made Annie's replies altogether too satisfactory to sound credible, the discomfort of Dr. Silla's look returned to haunt her.

Still, if Annie consented to give Ronnie up, this second letter *would* reach its destination in time; if not, Hilda, who often lit the kitchen fire in the mornings for her mother, would burn it on the top of the kitchen stove. After all, she would never see Dr. Silla again; nor would anyone suspect so famous a person of stealing test tubes or poisons on a complimentary visit to a foreign laboratory, and even if they did suspect her, Dr. Silla would be safely out of England.

Hilda was not doing Dr. Silla – or anyone else, except, of course, Ronnie – any harm! Perhaps she was not even doing Ronnie any real harm. Ronnie was so blindly selfish, and so cruelly false, that probably being dead would, in the long run, be less trouble even to himself than being alive. Poor Ronnie had to take a lot of trouble to get what he wanted. He had to concentrate to the highest pitch of his terrific, slippery wits, in order to carry off by trickery what he could quite easily have earned by a little unassuming merit. Ronnie really had an excellent brain; but he used it only to beat his fellows, and his charms were what he mainly counted on to beat them with.

Hilda had never known the real Ronnie until once, having grasped this elemental fact about him, she showed his charms up. The bare memory of how Ronnie had turned upon her, as dangerously as a rattlesnake, made her shiver. Ronnie was not even a very good friend; and people who are not even very good friends make terrible enemies.

If Hilda could make Annie realize what the real Ronnie was like, Annie would give him up fast enough! The trouble was that the real Ronnie was far too clever to come out into the open unless it paid him. Hilda could tell Annie just what he was like, but bare assertions are never convincing; nor is sadistic cruelty an easy thing to prove, since none of its manifestations take place except in the strictest privacy. Ronnie surrounded his victims with an atmosphere like poison gas, but when you came right down to it – and Annie being wildly in love with him, would be certain *to* come right down to it – what had Ronnie done to Hilda? Spirits do not show bruises.

At last Hilda heard them coming. First the happy voices a long way off; then at the turn of the road whispers and low laughter; then only their footsteps; and a pause before the gate clicked. Ronnie always used to kiss Hilda before they came in – in the shadow of a stunted lilac bush. He used to say they must have a last "outdoor kiss," since "indoor kisses" were a different and inferior species.

There was a long pause before the gate clicked, and the key turned in the latch.

Ronnie and Annie were very late, it was nearly one o'clock, so they came in quietly.

The stairs creaked; Ronnie's footsteps stopped at his door. Again a pause, while Hilda's heart leapt and sank, as if she had been running beyond her strength. The last few stairs Annie tiptoed up alone. But Ronnie waited to shut his door until he heard her open the door of Hilda's room.

"Oh, you've got the light still on!" Annie said, rather reproachfully. "I thought you'd be off to sleep long ago!"

It was awkward, Hilda thought, to have to talk so quietly about such vital things, but otherwise Father and Mother might hear through the thin cheap boards, even though they were good sleepers.

Annie looked very white and tired – as well she

might be, for she had worked hard all day, and had had far too long an evening. She was almost cross.

What she wanted was a good night's rest, and she was not going to get it!

Hilda's heart filled with compunction – even her wrongs faded. It was so usual for her to spare Annie, that she hardly knew how to do anything else *but* spare Annie! All her dramatizations failed her. She saw she was not going to make even a good beginning.

Still there was no other time to convince Annie, and Hilda had the sort of mind that carries out almost automatically what it has once decided upon.

"Look here, Annie," Hilda whispered in an urgent voice (she found it extremely tiresome to keep up in a whisper), "I've got something I *must* say to you!"

"What – to-night?" Annie answered rather too loudly. "Oh, I *can't* talk now, Hilda! I'm dead beat! I couldn't listen to the King! I couldn't really! I just want to lie down, and be dead to the world!"

Annie began to drag off her things, and throw them about on the floor as usual; then she scrambled into her pyjamas, and hurled herself onto her bed, without so much as washing her hands, let alone brushing her teeth. "Do turn out the light, Hilda!" she grumbled, the switch being just as near her as it was near Hilda. Hilda turned it out.

"I'm sorry, Annie," she said, trying to be sweet about it; "I can see you're tired – I'm truly sorry; but you've got to listen. I won't be any longer than I can help!"

"What's up?" Annie asked grudgingly. "Father got the sack? War on? Cut it as short as you can! Marlene was grand to-night, and so was Ronnie's club, but I've had enough of everything except sleep!"

"Enough of Ronnie!" Hilda thought, with a queer reproachful feeling, as if Annie was wronging Ronnie by being so tired. "Enough of Ronnie!" but she did not let the words pass her lips. Instead she murmured after a pause, making her lowered voice sound as gentle as she could: "Annie, we've been tremendous pals, haven't we – always? There's a good deal I'd do for you – more than for anyone else! You believe that, don't you?"

There was a queer rigidity about the slim outline of Annie's figure under the sheet; and when she answered Hilda her voice was toneless. "I suppose so," she admitted ungraciously. "Oh, for God's sake cut it short, can't you, Hilda?" Annie lay crouched up and turned away from Hilda, as if to hide herself; and speaking to the back of Annie's head made it difficult to begin what Hilda wanted to say.

"Annie, I *have* to say this – I have to ask it – do

you love Ronnie?" Perhaps it was silly to ask this question *first*, but Hilda knew Annie so well – and much depended upon how Annie answered it. If she did not take Ronnie seriously, nothing further need take place. Annie had had a great many boy friends in the past. Was Ronnie only one more of them, or was there, as Hilda feared, a fixity of Annie's versatile heart upon Ronnie's image?

Annie said, more crossly still, "What a silly question. Why shouldn't I go about with Ronnie – like I have with all my other boy friends?"

"Well – but is he – *like* those others?" Hilda persisted.

Annie made no direct answer, she thumped her pillow and said "Damn!"

Hilda knew then that Annie *did* love him. "Annie," she said desperately, without tact or dignity, and not at all as she had planned to say it, "you mustn't–you just *mustn't* love Ronnie! You don't know what it would let you in for – I do! He isn't true! He doesn't really love anyone but himself! He wants to see how much you'll give him for nothing – for nothing, Annie!"

There was a long pause, then Annie asked in a suspicious, unfriendly voice: "How do *you* know what Ronnie's like so well – you hardly ever speak to him? You think you know everything, but you don't! It's none of your business how much we like each other!"

"Ah, but you see it *is*," Hilda exclaimed passionately. "It *is* my business! He's been my lover; that's how I know what he's like!"

"What d'you mean by *lover?*" Annie demanded irritably. "Some girls think the postman's their lover if he knocks twice!"

"I mean what I say," Hilda repeated firmly. "Ronnie was really my lover – like a husband – he was mine! I'm sorry if I shock you, but it was the only way I could have him! It'll be the only way *you* can! And what I'm telling you is – that it isn't worth it! He treated me once as he's treating you now; and he'll cheat you as he cheated me! Sooner or later! It'll kill you, Annie!"

The words sprang past her lips without her meaning to say them. They seemed to pop out like hot nails pop out of burning wood.

Annie lay quite flat – without stirring – but every atom of her listened.

For a long time neither of them spoke, then Annie said in a stifled voice: "So that's what *you* say, is it? It isn't what Ronnie told me."

"What did – Ronnie – tell you?" Hilda asked. She

sat up perfectly straight. Her back seemed made of some unbendable, stiff substance – and her words came as slowly as if she had to dive for them under the weight of water. "What – did – Ronnie – tell you, Annie?"

Annie refused to answer; she remained as still as if she were shamming dead, and Hilda suddenly leaned over her and shook her. "If you hurt me, I shall call Ronnie!" Annie whispered fiercely.

It was unbelievable that Annie should suppose Hilda could *want* to hurt her! It was also unbelievable, but a fact, that Hilda had actually shaken her!

Hilda moved back into her own bed and took her former upright position, saying less firmly: "I won't, of course, hurt you! But I have a right to know what I asked! And why did you pretend *not* to know – if Ronnie really had already told you – everything!"

Annie too sat up, but she put both pillows behind her, and leaned back against them. "He said," Annie whispered vindictively into the kindly dark, "you wouldn't let him alone! He couldn't help what happened! He said he hated it, really! But he couldn't help it. He's a man! I understand – but you, you've never known men! You *made* him make love to you! But you didn't even know you *were* making him! You hadn't that much sense! It just shows! It wasn't even –

love! Ronnie's not my lover — not like that — but he's *in* love with me, that's why I have the whip hand. I don't go losing my head over men like that! Ronnie'll have to marry me — or get out! He knows that. I don't know yet which he'll do, but you've just *got* to leave us alone! I didn't tell you I knew about you before, though Ronnie told me ages ago, because I believe in keeping one's mouth shut when you're shocked — and I *was* shocked, I can tell you, to find my own sister behaving like — well, you know!" Annie's voice trailed off into the dark.

There seemed for a while nothing *but* the dark. Hilda never moved — her body went from hot to cold — from shivering cold to burning hot — her woman's body, that had known all the moods of passion — its ecstasies, its terrors, its weariness, and the completion of its joy.

The child's body beside her knew none of these things, but it might be that Annie's mind was wiser than her own! Had Hilda made a mistake from the first? Was it true that Ronnie had never — in any real sense — wanted her? Had she, Hilda, forced the pace of a thing that, until Ronnie urged it upon her, had no real existence for her? But suddenly, through the cold waves of her self-mistrust, flashed this one new fact — Ronnie *had* given her away! He told Annie!

This thing that he once said to Hilda was unbelievable for any man – let alone a gentleman – to do, Ronnie had done; he had given Hilda away to Annie! Nothing that Ronnie said had ever been true – so why should it be true that he had never loved Hilda? It was obviously easier to say it than to say that he had stopped loving Hilda – easier and a good deal more effective.

Hilda said more quietly and with no particular resentment – for after all, Annie could not help being shocked, she had spent three years in a convent school; and the sisters taught her among other things how to *be* shocked – "Annie, darling, think for a moment! You wouldn't have liked Ronnie to talk like – like that of you, to me, would you? Even if it *was* true! And you wouldn't have wished me to believe it! Besides you know quite well, I should *never* have believed it! To be his lover is one thing, but to *force* him to be my lover is quite another! It is not true! It took me quite a long time to – to love Ronnie like that! I hadn't ever wanted it. I only wanted to please him. He said if I wouldn't be, he couldn't go on staying here; and he's not strong – he liked being here – and he's very poor! We do make him terribly comfortable, Mums and I! So you see, that's how it happened! I don't think I forced anything – except, a little – myself! You do believe me, don't you, Annie?"

"No!" said Annie. "I don't believe you! I think it was disgusting of you! And now I'm going to sleep!" Annie dragged her pillows down again, curled up once more with her back to Hilda, and, after a few minutes, Hilda could tell by her quiet breathing that Annie actually *was* asleep.

The scene was over. It had not once gone like this in any of those vivid satisfactory rehearsals!

"She isn't *really* brutal!" Hilda told herself, after a long strained pause. "She's just young. Besides, I'd forgotten Ronnie! I'd forgotten he wouldn't wait for me to put my case. It always had to be *his* case. And he thought I wouldn't ever put mine at all! But if I did, he took care that it wouldn't sound probable – after his! God in Heaven, how I hate him! Oh, Ronnie! Ronnie!"

The walls and floor of the room seemed to thin out till there was nothing but that familiar lean young figure – whose every movement, every line, Hilda knew by heart, lying once more beside her, his head upon her breast! To forget – to betray – to replace – how cheap a way of loving!

"I can't help it," Hilda said to herself in the dark – as if she were speaking to some responsible intelligent person, like that lecturer for instance, whom she had to convince before her own mind could feel wholly at its ease, "I can't help it! He *mustn't* do it again! Not to Annie! He mustn't ever do it again!"

Hilda lay down at last, her body stretched very straight, without relaxing a single muscle. She felt as if she were holding the bed poised in the air – perhaps the whole house – perhaps the earth itself, by her taut muscles. She could not let go. Nor was the feeling wholly anger. It was a sort of bitter responsibility. Some people believed in God – and some in other people – and some in themselves; but Hilda could not quite say what she believed in. Only she knew that she could not leave things alone, when she was sure they would hurt someone she loved.

Annie must be saved from Ronnie. Perhaps she didn't want to be – but that was only because Annie did not know what *not* being saved from Ronnie would be like – and she must never find out!

The best plan, now, was simply to do that fantastic, incredible thing she had felt completely released from doing earlier in the evening.

Hilda had said to herself quite firmly before Annie came in: "It'll come out all right! I'll take that letter round to the Lab. on my way to the office!" And now she did not for a long time say anything to herself. Nor did she rehearse any more what was going to happen. She tried not to remember that kind, confident look the lecturer had given her, as if she knew that Hilda was a reliable person; but Hilda stayed awake remembering it – until the milkman came.

Chapter 6

WHEN Hilda woke up after an hour's troubled sleep, she went straight downstairs, lit the kitchen fire and burned Dr. Silla's letter to the Laboratory, on the top of the stove.

They would expect Dr. Silla now at eleven o'clock; and they would get Hilda.

After this step, Hilda felt distinctly better. Of course, she assured herself, the whole thing was nonsense.

As a child she had had day-dreams of performances far beyond her reach, or even her desire.

She had not, in those far-distant days, made any attempt to put these day-dreams to the test of reality. Although she had once gone so far as to build a house in a tree; but she had not lived in it. She was not going to poison Ronnie, that was the purest fantasy; her visit to the Laboratory need never come to any such drastic issue.

Why not divert her mind by a clever trick, which would give her a sense of power over an unendurable situation? Walking about in the possession of a lethal weapon, she would no longer feel this awful sense of defeat which was breaking up her life. She would know, too, that if Ronnie put Annie to the torture, she had the means to stop it.

Hilda did not like the idea of not posting Dr. Silla's letter. The foreign lecturer had made a very good and deep impression upon Hilda, and it seemed mean to let a customer down. Still, Hilda was not going to do Dr. Silla any real harm. Quite probably Hilda would get away with a poison (or a tube containing lethal germs such as Ronnie had often described to her) without anyone being the wiser. If they found out, they would not be likely to suspect a famous colleague from abroad of being a thief; and if they did suspect her, they could not get hold of her, as by that time Dr. Silla would be out of England.

Beyond getting into the Laboratory with the card Dr. Silla had given her for the lecture (fortunately they had only glanced at it at the door, and let Hilda keep it) Hilda had made no plans.

Already she felt the better for having burned the letter; the conflict within her mind began to die down.

Apparently, however, Hilda did not look any better, for her mother said to her at breakfast, "Hilda, I've never seen you with such lines under your eyes, I'm downright worried about you!"

Instead of answering, as most grown-up daughters would have automatically answered their intruding mothers, with "Nonsense! I feel perfectly all right. I wish you wouldn't fuss!" Hilda replied, after a moment's pause:

"I don't feel any too grand, Mums, and that's a fact! I was wondering, since it's Friday anyhow, whether I couldn't run down to Aunt Edith's this afternoon, for a long week-end? I've only got a little law work on hand, so I could shut the office at two o'clock, and come up when I liked Monday."

Her mother looked both surprised and gratified at Hilda's prompt acceptance of her warning.

"You couldn't do better, Hilda," she said cordially. "Of course your Aunt Edith, living alone, and having plenty of room in that big bungalow of hers, doesn't *like* being taken by surprise! Still she keeps a full girl, though she could perfectly well do with a char on Saturdays, as I've often told her! I never have seen why those Fenchurches hold their noses higher than the Catesbys! If I come from a tradesman's family — which I've never denied — your father's own brother sailed before the mast, and you can't get away from that, can you? What I say is an aunt's an aunt, even if she calls herself a tutor in a training college!"

"Well, Aunt Edith *is* a tutor in a training college," Hilda reminded her mother a little impatiently, "and all that's completely bourgeois anyhow, as I've often told you! It'll be a classless world soon and then nobody'll mind what their families are! Still, I had thought of wiring Aunt Edith on my way to the office; it won't cost more than ninepence, and it's no use getting her all ruffled up! We can give Annie another half-hour's sleep, can't we, without her getting into a row for it? Poor kid, she came in awfully late last night, all tired out!"

"I shall tell her off for it," remarked Mr. Fenchurch, who had just come down rather late himself. "A girl of her age sleeping the clock round! Annie don't take her work seriously enough, that's what it is! Why, at her age I was up at six o'clock winter and summer alike, an hour both ways to and from the factory, and three miles to the station on my bike! I don't hold with these late evenings either! They don't seem right for a young girl like our Annie! I really wonder, Mother, you don't put a stop to them! Pictures are over at eleven, and twenty minutes is time enough to get home from the Fulham Palace. Besides the money! Somebody's got to pay for it, haven't they? And nobody in this house can suppose it's Master Ronnie! It's pleasure, pleasure, all the time, with these young people! What's more," Mr. Fenchurch went on, rapidly winding himself up into a climax of emotion that made him slop his coffee over into his saucer and threatened the tablecloth, "I *won't* have this young Ronnie playing round with one of my girls at all hours of the night; how do I know that they ever *went* to the cinema at all?" And he stabbed his fried egg so savagely that he had to mop it up with a crust of bread, or lose half its value.

"If they could really do anything to stop it," Hilda found herself thinking wearily, "I might tell them, and get Ronnie kicked out. But they'd just fluster up and down again, and never get on with the job! Besides if Ronnie *did* leave the house, Annie'd only meet him outside, and not let on about it! Telling them wouldn't get us anywhere, and upset them both to hell into the bargain! Better keep quiet about it, and soothe the old boy down, I suppose."

"They went to the pictures all right, Dad," she told her father reassuringly. "Annie said Marlene was grand!"

"Oh, well," replied her father, unreasonably mollified by the mere name of his favourite star, "I dare say I'll take a look at her new film myself on Saturday. If you *know* they went there, that's different! I'll take the *Mirror* with me, Hilda, and mind you remember to bring your mother home a *Mail* and not that red rag of a *Herald*. I won't have that paper under my roof – whether you're of age or not!"

Hilda looked warningly at her father under her thick red eyebrows, but she rose quietly, and even dropped a kiss on his bald head, for somehow or other the mere thought that he could not stop her doing what she wanted, about the *Herald* or about anything else, endeared him to her. She used to be afraid of standing up to her father when she was a child, but it was different now. She knew that there was really nothing to stand up to.

Above her father's exposed and shining crown, she gave her mother the look of a fellow conspirator signalling an action, to which no attention is to be drawn.

Her mother had often said, "*Let* things happen, without mentioning them beforehand! Talk *after* a thing's done is a lot different from talk before, the stuffing's gone out of it!"

Hilda thought of this saying now, and decided to let the subject of her visit to Aunt Edith come out afterwards. It was a good idea to get well away with those tubes in her pocket, but no need to make a song and dance about it!

She ran swiftly upstairs to pack her bag, and moved so quietly about the room that she did not even wake Annie; then she waited a few minutes after she had heard the front gate click behind her father, before she slipped out into the street, on her way to her own office.

Fortunately for Hilda, Dr. Manning Foster, the chief of the Pathological Department, a man both shrewd and hard-headed, decided, an hour before her arrival, to thrust aside the international courtesy put upon him by the hospital to which his Laboratory was attached, and leave it to his assistant, Dr. Adrian Laing, to receive the Czech visitor.

Manning Foster had three reasons which seemed to him excellent for avoiding such a duty.

He disapproved of women doctors – if they were inefficient, for the sake of their patients; if they were efficient, for the sake of their male rivals.

He disliked foreign doctors for much the same basic reasons, outside of their own countries, where he did not mind their doing what they liked.

Nor was Manning Foster at all sure that Dr. Silla

was prominent enough to exact international courtesy.

Central Europe might know her; but London certainly did not.

"What are this confounded woman's credentials?" he demanded irritably of his second. "*I've* never heard of her before, have you? Hospital in Prague – that's the place with all those towers, isn't it, crossing bridges – capital of Czechoslovakia, one of those new Wilson countries! *Is* there such a thing as a good Czech neurologist?"

Adrian Laing shook his head doubtfully. He had never even heard of a good Czech; besides, he mixed Czechs up with Rumanians; and he had been told on quite good authority that Rumanians were both unscientific and immoral.

"I don't see that a foreign doctor has any right to lecture to the British public," Manning Foster fumed on, in a voice that grew more and more aggressive, as he watched one after the other of his favourite prejudices sail out upon the sea of his own eloquence. "If *we* lecture, even in our own hospitals, nobody comes to hear us, unless they're forced to! They say this woman's lectures have drawn crowds – and you can see for yourself the sickening way the papers take it up!

"A performing seal means more to the British public than a piece of decent research that might scotch typhoid! Neurologist too – what's she got to do with psychiatry? Far better leave that alone and stick to glands. We're safe there – as far as they go. I never have believed in letting patients know anything about themselves, either! They get mixed up and start criticizing *us!*

"These chattering psychiatrists do a lot of harm – they go round pointing out to people they aren't ill at all, or could get better if they chose; and then *we* get belated cancer cases beyond operating point; or silly women with mumps thinking they've got a sex complex! Still, somebody'll have to take the woman on, as the Hospital's asked it!"

Manning Foster looked entreatingly at Adrian Laing; Laing would do as he was told, of course, but would he *suggest* doing it? That was what Manning Foster wanted! His conscience had not been wholly appeased by his own eloquence; he knew quite well that he ought to show the woman round his Laboratory himself.

"I'll do whatever you wish, of course," his second said unhappily, for he was a shy young man, and thought either a Rumanian or a Czech lady doctor might be quite beyond his powers, "but don't you think perhaps you *had* better stay, yourself? You see, the papers might be down on us, for lack of international courtesy, if she *was* somebody or other, you know – and it was only *me*, I mean."

You never knew quite where you were with Manning Foster, Adrian Laing thought, for at this appeal the big man whirled right round and began dragging off his linen coat. "No! You'll do perfectly," he stated sharply. "Just take her over the Lab. Show her the new Centrifuge and some of my specimens. That new variety of Shiga's bacillus is just the thing! By the by, they telephoned from the Hospital this morning to say the woman's dead, the man died yesterday, and the children can't hold out – I knew they couldn't, but what they wanted to ring us up for, the Lord only knows. It's not our job whether people die or not; all we've got to settle is what they die of! That beautiful culture doesn't leave much doubt about it in this case, poor souls! The Health Ministry, or whatever they call themselves, might do something about those pork-pies though, in hot weather, set in plate-glass windows in the sun! God knows what the stuff they call '*aspic*' is made of! Clotted up under a tough crust with no ventilation! Always the same thing at the end of a hot summer!

"If this Government were *really* national, instead of a lot of wobbling old women all holding on to their own pockets and begging Hitler and Mussolini to let 'em keep what's inside 'em, they'd pay us to examine the urine of pregnant women, and get on with this mortality leakage at childbirth – that's what we want a Ministry of Health for, isn't it?"

Adrian Laing nodded unhappily. Would this foreign lady even speak English, he was asking himself? Did Rumanians talk French? He could read French, of course, but would he be expected to speak it?

"What do our Government officials care," Manning Foster boomed tirelessly on, while washing his hands carefully with carbolic soap, "as long as their golf links are kept up, and their own wives sterile at convenient intervals? By the by, Laing, have you been to any of this truculent virgin's lectures?"

Adrian Laing privately thought his chief a little unfair; how did they know that this lady *was* truculent? Some women were quiet. His mother, for instance, had been one of the quiet ones; and Adrian had profited by it.

"To tell you the truth, I haven't! Ought I to have gone?" Adrian replied, seeing by his chief's face that he had done well to abstain from attending any of Dr. Silla's lectures.

"Sensible fellow!" Manning Foster beamed at him across the towel. "Those are my golf clubs in the corner, aren't they? Tell her I'm frightfully sorry, but had to attend an important medical conference; there *is* one, I believe, sometime this afternoon. You might just show her those slides of the disseminated sclerosis I did last year – they show up rather well. I could have done some valuable research work on that line if I'd got government support for it. They think you ought to settle every bacillus in the universe for the price of a tram fare! And call that 'endowing Research'! That pituitary we made sections out of, the other day, would bear looking at too; and get Simmons to show her any good plates you can think of – besides my own, I mean, of course. What's that? Have to talk French to her? Nonsense, if she knows enough English to ask her way here, she must know enough for you to show her round! Besides, what do you suppose she lectured in – French? With those crowds to hear her? Not on your life she didn't! So long."

Hilda did not know that the large handsome man in plus-fours, with a bag full of golf clubs, who dashed past her down the steps and hailed a taxi, was a fatal obstacle being providentially removed from her path; but she did say to herself, as the keen blue eyes flashed a scrutinizing glance at her: "Well, thank goodness I shan't have to talk to *that* man this morning!"

Chapter 7

HILDA felt as if she were hanging in space, with nothing beneath her but air. Surely the first word she tried to speak to the grave-eyed young man in the long white linen coat would be her doom?

Not all Ronnie's casual talk of microscopes and sterilizers could save her from the pitfalls of her fundamental ignorance.

This specialized room was in itself too expert, and this terrifying young man too workmanlike, not to force her into self-exposure.

Fortunately for Hilda, the young man himself was equally nervous.

Adrian Laing was always afraid of women he did not know; and a foreign woman, younger and better-looking than he had anticipated – who might be expecting him to talk French to her – was a paralyzing spectacle.

Even Hilda, after the first awful moment, saw that Adrian was in a state of terror. "The more frightened I keep him, the less frightened I need be *of* him!" she told herself with desperate courage. But in spite of this reassurance, she heard Adrian's voice, when at last he managed to speak to her, as a drowning man might hear a shout across the water.

"My name is Adrian Laing," the young man told Hilda diffidently. "I'm afraid I can't speak French properly. We thought – we hoped – my chief said, perhaps you had lectured in English?"

Hilda nodded. "Yes," she said at last, hoping that her English would not sound too good, "that is true. I speak English."

Adrian's face cleared a little. He was an honest, pleasant-looking young man, Hilda thought; he held his well-made body a little stiffly, as if he was not used to letting it do exactly what he wanted. The eyes that met Hilda's were neither intimate nor magnetic; Ronnie's eyes were both. Still, when he smiled Ronnie looked like a bantering angel; whereas this young man, if he smiled at all, did so with reluctance, as if he were letting go something that he disliked parting from.

"I'm afraid my chief," he told Hilda, "won't be able to meet you. There is an important conference on in London just now, and Dr. Manning Foster feels he ought not to miss a session. Of course, he very much regrets not being able to show you over his Laboratory."

Hilda smiled vaguely; she looked away from the young man, who in this fraction of time had ceased to be the most terrifying thing in the room and become instead the least terrifying. It would be as well, she thought, to accustom herself to the strange-looking things she saw about her, before she began to talk of them.

The Laboratory was a long narrow room, with a row of white-tiled sinks at one end of it.

Down its length ran a double line of backless benches, with Bunsen burners set above them at convenient intervals. There was a large sterilizer in one corner, and a noisy centrifuge spun swiftly behind its glass wall, close to where Hilda stood.

Midway between the benches stood one or two microscopes, which Hilda recognized with relief to be microscopes, though she could not quite remember how to deal with them. There were glass cases against the wall, with rather odd things or portions of things inside them; and there were several young men at work before the benches, who unobtrusively disappeared, or vanished into inner rooms, before Hilda had had time to be introduced to them.

It was a relief to her, to find herself alone in the hot light room with Dr. Laing; and it was a still greater relief when he turned off the violently revolving centrifuge.

"Now we can hear ourselves talk," he explained to her; "the little one over there doesn't matter, but this big fellow (I must admit we are rather proud of him) *is* noisy! There is only one other like it, in California!"

Hilda was not sure how advisable it was for them to be able to hear each other speak, but she was quite sure that she was glad there was only one other such instrument in the world. She felt less terrified now that the whirling so close to her head had stopped. The worst of a dog-fight, she thought, is the noise the dogs make when they fight – if they only bit, no one but themselves would be the wiser. She and Dr. Laing would certainly (if they fought at all) be noiseless fighters.

An inspiration occurred to Hilda, and she said: "I must confess to you my English is weak! If I say something too stupid please forgive me. I can understand all that you say to me, but my lectures – dare I tell you? – I had to learn them by heart!"

Adrian became kinder still, he seemed thoroughly to understand the situation, and launched himself, with sudden assurance, into explaining everything in the Laboratory.

He might not be at his ease socially with a strange girl, but he knew a good deal – even more perhaps than his chief did – about the treasures of his own Laboratory; the strange girl too was not only a strange girl. She was another doctor.

Hilda made a good listener, so good that Adrian found it quite easy to believe in her intelligence; fortunately Hilda had a mechanical mind, and had always mended her own typewriter; this helped her, after her first blind terror sank away from her, to see what *not* to ask about an instrument. She bent down to look through the lens of a microscope as if she did not expect it to go off like a pistol.

She had to remind herself, though, not to show too much interest, for looking through a really good microscope for the first time has a fascination that it is difficult to hide. Hilda excused herself by saying that in Czechland they could not afford such remarkably fine lenses.

Once it flashed through her mind that if it had not been for Ronnie himself, she could not have carried off this impersonation as a doctor at all!

She had listened to every word Ronnie had ever let drop about his work, simply because it bore some relation to Ronnie; and she thought with a pang that she was putting the knowledge she had won from him to a strange use!

Only once, over an instrument that automatically divided certain ingredients into their constituent parts, did Hilda make a bad blunder. She asked a question the answer to which, she saw in a flash by Adrian's bewildered eyes, she should certainly have known.

However, she succeeded in laughing off her question as a language blunder; and from that moment Hilda sheered off instruments. Cultures, she suggested, were what she most longed to investigate. This brought her to Adrian's pet subject; and at length to the pride of the Laboratory — the Shiga bacilli!

Adrian slipped a slide under the lens of the most powerful of the microscopes, and Hilda leaned eagerly over it, listening to his explanation with an interest that Adrian found quite extraordinarily flattering.

"It is highly toxic, of course," Adrian finished. "The contents of one of these tubes could kill a family; indeed considerably less has already killed a whole family. The culture from the feces has grown surprisingly stronger than the original bacillus." Hilda gave a queer little sigh, and stood up straight. This was all she wanted to know. One of these tubes would do. It would be safer to take two, in case one got broken.

There were, she could see, plenty of other poisons in the Laboratory, and they were quite get-at-able. Glass-stoppered bottles stood about on some of the benches, any one of which might contain all the poison she needed; and perhaps of an even more instantaneous kind than the contents of the tube which had killed a whole family. But how was Hilda to know which bottle, or how much to take from it? It was obviously wiser not to ask questions about poisons, whereas it was only natural, and Hilda saw that Adrian took it as only natural, to say after a pause, "What food do you suppose carried the original poison?"

"Well, the source of bacteria is always difficult to follow," Adrian replied without hesitation. "We never think tinned foods so dangerous as people suppose; the treatment of the tins has been carried out so successfully of late years that you can practically preserve anything. If people take ordinary precautions after the tin has been opened, nothing much should go wrong. One might advise people to keep off the acids, perhaps, but I can't say we've had any trouble from them. It's generally those gingered-up meats in third-rate restaurants, or kept in dirty larders, that cause trouble. Besides patients seldom come to hospital quickly enough, nor have they accurate memories of what they have just eaten. Our English poor seldom keep their food beyond the meal they buy it for — but if it's been kept originally for too long, that of course doesn't help them! Naturally we have nothing to do with the lethal side of what is sent to us, beyond reporting what the bacillus is.

"Sometimes I rather wish we *had;* whatever brings one into direct contact with human beings has a special value! Still, half the fun of a laboratory is its exactness — and you don't get exactness very often from human beings, do you? I must say we're lucky here. We've got a splendid chief to work under, he's the most thorough man in London — nothing escapes Manning Foster's eye!"

Hilda thought that in that case she had been spared a good deal by not having had to meet Manning Foster's eye, but she said aloud:

"You are yourself a very good guide! I could desire no better!" Which sent the young man off blushing.

"Our poor," Hilda said reflectively, thinking that perhaps at this moment the foreign element had better be reintroduced, "seldom eat meat, and the rich

— though we have not so many rich — feed carefully; therefore we do not have many cases of food poisoning. Also in Czechland we have many cows; and the poorest of us drink great quantities of milk. You remember how the circle of the Borgias found drinking milk, after the honour of dining with that celebrated family, conducive to longer living?" For a moment Hilda forgot her own relationship to the family in question, and gave Adrian a beautiful and friendly smile.

"Why, she's — beautiful!" Adrian said to himself; and then suddenly Hilda remembered her relationship to the Borgias, and her face darkened and stiffened into positive pain. "It is her pity," Adrian told himself. "She is thinking of that whole family I told her about!" And he felt more admiration for Hilda than ever; for by now Hilda was perfectly safe. Nothing that she could do or say failed to add to Adrian Laing's admiration for her. "We send our reports to the police as soon as possible," he told her reassuringly, "and they inspect all the food shops in the vicinity, and confiscate anything suspect. I don't believe anyone else will suffer from our 'Shiga'!"

Hilda shivered; she made no answer. She saw, for a moment, the miracle of Ronnie's body, once dearer to her than anything on earth, pitilessly invaded by a tasteless, sightless germ, harried by unknown pains into ultimate darkness. Her sight grew dim; but she could not drive the terrible image out of her mind.

"Shall I show you one of Manning Foster's pituitary gland sections? They're frightfully interesting," Adrian's voice, pleasant and diffident, broke in upon her like a rescue.

"If it is not too great a trouble," Hilda murmured. She drew herself stiffly away from the side of the microscope, but as she passed the Petrie dish that contained the Shiga tubes, mechanically her mind recounted them.

Adrian took a long time explaining to Hilda the pituitary gland sections; and then suggested their going into a room where the plates were kept in order to show Hilda Manning Foster's disseminated sclerosis.

"I am so sorry," Hilda exclaimed. "I should so much have liked to see such a thing. I am much interested in disseminated sclerosis, but I must telephone to a friend. It is already later than I promised, and I must confess I find it difficult to telephone in English. This is a trunk call! I find them the worst — for with them, I must also try to understand what the telephone people themselves say!"

"Your English is most frightfully good," Adrian assured Hilda with warmth, "but I'd be delighted to put in your call for you. You have only to tell me what district, and what number!"

Once more Hilda smiled that slow, enthralling smile that lit her sombre eyes, till they seemed to Adrian the very texture and spirit of light. A moment later, Hilda found herself alone, with only the sound of the drip from the taps and the Bunsens sizzling; but her heart beat loudly in her ears, as if it were an approaching footstep.

There was no one else in the long narrow room. She could take what she wanted.

Hilda moved back swiftly to the Petrie dish, where the Shiga tubes lay in their neat rows. She picked out two, pushing the fragile line neatly together again with a careful finger-tip.

The tubes were in her bag now, between layers of cotton wool, and she was back again staring with sightless eyes at Manning Foster's sections of pituitary glands. She could hear Ronnie's voice saying to her, with that slight twist of boastfulness that all his words carried: "I could carry off any poison I liked, from our Lab. – and no one be any the wiser. Of course they're supposed to count the tubes once a day at least – it's one of the Lab. boys' business – but I happen to know they often forget to do it!"

One of the "Lab. boys" came in at that moment,

and stared at Hilda; her heart missed a beat; but he did not go near the tubes; and a moment later Adrian rejoined her. He was distressed because they had not been able to get an answer from the number Hilda had given him.

Hilda, however, was almost embarrassingly grateful. Her friend, and her friend's maid, must both be out, she explained, but Adrian had enabled her to keep her word, and that was all that mattered. It was a pity her friend had not been in, because she left England to-night, and now would not be able to see her again; still it could not be helped!

"I was wondering," Adrian suggested with eager humility, "if perhaps some day I couldn't get to Prague on a holiday – it's where you live, isn't it – and then possibly you would allow me to call on you?"

Hilda looked at him for a long time with quite extraordinary gravity. Her silence seemed almost hostile, and Adrian began wretchedly to ask himself if his suggestion had carried – to a native of Czechoslovakia – any insulting flavour.

At last Hilda answered him with kindness, though her voice carried a hint of finality. "I am afraid that cannot be!" she said slowly. "For I am going almost immediately to America, where I have been offered an appointment. I hope that we may meet again sometime, though – upon the other side of the Atlantic!" And she held out her hand in a gesture that Adrian had to accept as a farewell.

"If I had any sense," he told himself afterwards, "I might have asked her out to lunch! Now I shall *never* see her again!" For Hilda had disappeared with an almost terrifying suddenness. She had smiled though, as she reached the door, as if it was not Adrian that she was hurrying so briskly away from.

But Adrian would not have seen Hilda again, in any recognizable sense, even if he had sat opposite to her two hours later in the train; for by that time Hilda had made away with any trace of her extremely careful make-up; even the arch of her eyebrows was gone. Her sedate black dress was replaced by a skimpy and sleeveless blue cotton one; and she wore no hat.

She could no longer be mistaken for a foreign doctor upon a lecture tour; she looked like what she was —a typist on a holiday, and not one of the grandest kind of typists either; but Hilda carried the same hand-bag, and in it were two of Adrian's most prized Shiga bacilli tubes.

Leaning back in the corner of an empty third-class

carriage, Hilda's mind relaxed. There might be flaws in what she had done, but she could not remember any, and she could do nothing about them now, if there were. Her suit-case was safely on the rack above her head. She could get rid of her make-up at Aunt Edith's; and it was natural to take a black dress for Sunday, although Hilda thought she certainly would not wear it — not quite so soon anyhow! Dr. Silla, as an inhabitant of England, no longer existed, and Czechoslovakia was a long way from Aunt Edith's.

It was a warm day, and Hilda had not had any food for a long time, but she might be able to buy a banana at a passing station. She looked out of the window at the pleasant little hurrying fields; some of them were empty already, but others were still bright with harvest.

The landscape was full of tranquillity and unaggressive strength; curiously enough it reminded Hilda of Dr. Silla herself, with her smiling, wise eyes, and that air she had of being at once too strong and too sane ever to do anyone any harm.

The relief Hilda felt at having accomplished her purpose began to dwindle.

"I shan't really *need* to do anything about those tubes!" Hilda told herself defensively. "Not at once

– not unless . . . ! It's only that I *could* do it now if I had to! It's such a comfort not to have to feel trapped any more!"

But supposing that she were to feel trapped once more – trapped into using the tubes, just as she had felt trapped into taking them?

Dr. Silla on her way to Dover, earlier in the day (for it was now half-past two, and the boat-train went at eleven) must have seen the same mellow oast-houses, the colour of pressed grapes, under the clear, colourless sky; and marvelled at the clustered red-cheeked apples in the Kentish orchards loading down their small, solid trees; but Dr. Silla would have enjoyed looking at them.

"I suppose I ought to have eaten something," Hilda told herself, "but I didn't somehow much like the look of that station food."

Again Hilda thought of Dr. Silla, and with something very like a pang. "It's silly," she told herself protestingly, "to mind so much about just *not* posting a letter! But I *do* mind it! I mind it more than pretending to be her; and I really did do that slow voice, and the stiff sort of way she talks, rather well! I mind about that letter more too than I mind anything that might – but of course, I don't suppose it will ever have to – happen, to those tubes!"

Hilda's mind skipped the word "poison" and the word "Ronnie."

She found, as many people have found before her, that she shrank from giving a name to what she meant to do.

Chapter 8

HILDA thought there was a good deal to be said for the cliffs round Dover on a fine August day, especially if you were alone with them. Aunt Edith had gone to Dover to shop; but they were to meet again at tea. She had been very kind in suggesting that Hilda should enjoy the sea air, in an undiluted form; still she would not like her to be late for tea.

There was no scenery as such — no hills, no streams, no trees, no feasts of architecture, no riot of colour; but the few cornfields unpunctured by bungalows shone a clear gold under a cloud-ringed patch of blue; above them invisible larks shot out delicious spurts of joy; and at the foot of the short white cliffs, the sea rustled in a friendly summer way. Neither sky nor sea were brilliantly blue, but they melted into each other in a pearly haze and every breath Hilda drew of the keen and gorgeous air filled her with physical vigour.

She was so nearly happy, when she found in a corner of a field a hedge to lean against unrobbed of honeysuckle, that her mind turned traitor and began to fling once more before her eyes insistent images of Ronnie. That was the worst of always associating joy with one particular person; the moment anything nice turned up you had to link it to them. Nor were these images of Ronnie particularly happy images.

It even occurred to Hilda, dragged back into the torment of memory, that there had been no hours of really happy intimacy with Ronnie to look back on. Their times together had always been permeated by fear – fear of seeming stupid – of failing to please – of hearing cruel words – or of those short bored sighs that Ronnie was an adept in turning into personal insults.

Hilda not only had had to bear her own faults, but she had soon become responsible for the faults of the uncertain universe: a wet day; a missed bus; a chance ache or pain – any form of postponement or disappointment that crossed Ronnie's path was promptly used by him as a weapon in the uneven game of passion – heads I win – tails you lose. Nor had there been – for Hilda, even in the days of their earliest rapture (when Ronnie's nature had seemed as unruffled as a summer's day), an hour without the weight of guilt. Hilda might think or say that she thought she had a right to take love as her own affair, and lie right and left to hide the fact that she had taken it; but she loved her home, her parents had never been aggressive obstacles to her growing will, she had always lived in a household that was without any settled habits of resentment. To keep from such a family all knowledge of an intense intimacy, out of their power to approve or to accept, – an intimacy balanced between ecstasy and torment, – and to show no outward sign of these conflicting emotions, had been a tightrope form of existence. Hilda knew that she ought by rights to have felt nothing but relief, when it was over; but she had always supposed that their love wasn't going to go on under such a pressure. She had not envisaged marriage; but Ronnie had always promised her that, directly he had finished his exams and started any form of practice, he would share a flat with Hilda – in St. John's Wood, for instance – as far as possible from anyone they knew, and that then their life would be a marvellous performance without jars or frets, concealments or postponements; so that they would not quarrel any more.

Of course it might not have worked out quite like this, Hilda acknowledged to herself, but the plan had shone — a vision of bliss — to lighten her thorny path; and now, instead of such a plan, there was nothing but this craving emptiness. Hilda had no goal and the future held only the certainty of seeing Annie caught in the same trap. Curiously enough Hilda felt no anger against Annie. She felt pain, but not a pain that roused in her any desire to retaliate. Annie, she thought dreamily, could not help despising her; and in a way was right to do so. Besides, her contempt was a sort of safeguard. If Annie despised Hilda for allowing Ronnie to be her lover presumably she would at least postpone, if not refuse, the same unstable arrangement.

Hilda realized that a love affair which only involves the imagination may be a disappointment — even a cruelly vivid disappointment; but at least Annie would escape the rapacity of a physical habit. A desire that has never been fulfilled is considerably less acute than one that has been fulfilled and then checked at the source.

The moment to intervene, — Hilda thought with sombre common sense, undeflected by the sweetness of the honeysuckle, – since she could not stop Annie's desires, was before they had become realities.

It was no use thinking that Annie could hold out for ever against Ronnie – however virtuous she thought she was. Heroines in books, who seldom live under the same roof as their lovers, can perhaps, if they have the temperament for it, remain permanently pure; warm-hearted, loving little girls like Annie do not come under this category. Nor had Ronnie any of that protective chivalry which makes heroes in fiction, however tempted, postpone their bliss, until marriage bells and family blessings have polished off all sense of sin.

Ronnie never stopped, until he had had everything that he wanted; and then what he stopped was wanting what he already possessed.

Hilda had tried to change Ronnie, as all lovers try to change the beloved; and had failed, as all lovers sooner or later fail.

She knew now that nothing could be expected from the sweet flintishness of his character, beyond its deceptive polish.

She had tried last night to change Annie, but that was more hopeless still. If Hilda had not been able to change a lover, she saw now that she was a fool to suppose she could change a sister.

An appeal to her parents would be worse than useless; it would simply precipitate a flirtation into a serious love affair. Ronnie would immediately be turned out of the house; Annie would be scolded – and being unhappy would soon fly to a source where happiness could be reached without scolding.

Ronnie roused to boiling point by criticism and frustration would make short work of both his own and Annie's scruples. To first take and then desert Annie would punish successfully the family that had dared to oppose his wishes.

What way was there then of saving Annie – short of removing Ronnie with finality? And what finality was within Hilda's power – but that which lurked serenely in her two little tubes?

It was a lovely evening; the turn of the tide sent little gusts of travelling shadow over the golden corn; the larks sang unhampered between nests and sky. Poison was hardly a suitable subject for such a setting; and Hilda turned her sick mind away from it, to Aunt Edith. Here was another experienced, older person – one whom Hilda had admired and relied on, since her earliest childhood. Might she not know some other way out of this dilemma?

Aunt Edith was sufficiently young to be trusted with a modern problem.

She was only thirty-eight and a lecturer in a training college.

Young girls – dozens of them – confided in her. She knew something about psychology. She was modern herself in an inconclusive way. She smoked continuously; and although she sometimes went to church, she had had a love affair with a married man.

Aunt Edith had explained to Hilda, rather laboriously, that the affair had not gone beyond a certain point.

The married man – after a good deal of brilliant argument; perhaps rather too much argument, for Aunt Edith was a great talker – had let the matter slide.

"We discussed it fully," Aunt Edith had explained to Hilda and to several other admiring young persons in whom she had sufficient confidence to present her case, "and decided to part. Morally we felt justified to love freely – but not ethically! We felt that we must act for the sake of the community."

"And she believes that stuff!" Hilda told herself enviously. "I suppose, though, it was the talk that put him off; besides he had a wife to fall back on anyhow!"

Still it was no use underrating Aunt Edith's basic intelligence. She had furnished her bungalow in an austere modern manner meant to represent the eighteenth century; and read all of Nietzsche and could quote T. S. Eliot and W. H. Auden without mixing them up.

Hilda had spent part of all her summer holidays with Aunt Edith and knew most of her friends – not the married man, of course; Aunt Edith had met him – and parted from him – on a cruise.

Last holidays had been the only failure in Hilda and Aunt Edith's intercourse. Hilda had been gloomy and irritable, carrying a thorn under her skin, and Aunt Edith had – very naturally and skilfully – tried to extract the thorn. Hilda had told her nothing; and had deeply resented Aunt Edith's having realized that she had something to be extracted.

Still curiously enough, Hilda felt quite differently now; not only was she without resentment towards her Aunt Edith, but she found herself for the first time since she and Ronnie were lovers actually wanting to tell someone else about him!

For one thing, if Aunt Edith really *had* any solution for the problem of getting Ronnie to give Annie up, no further measures need be taken. Those little tubes that were alternately a terror and a relief to Hilda could just be poured harmlessly away, down a closet, or opened into the measureless cleanliness of the sea; and even if Aunt Edith was less a source of wisdom than she was an innocent old maid, it would be a relief to Hilda to speak once of her love, before she decided to turn it into hate.

"Perhaps I could see it all differently," Hilda told herself, staring with hot dry eyes at the golden corn. "She might make me think of something else – something about Ronnie I haven't understood – that would help me not to *want* to kill him! Of course there isn't anything, because I've tried and tried – but perhaps I've tried too much – thinking of Ronnie is like adding up a column of figures and always getting sixpence out, and then someone comes along with a fresh eye and sees where the sixpence is, straight off! Besides when I've tried, I've always been *minding* – Aunt Edith could try, without caring a damn! I know she's got awfully little feeling – she's so intellectual and finds that a help. Of course I shan't mention a thing about the lecturer or the Laboratory – that woman must be in France by now. I wish I was! I wish I'd ever been able to go anywhere – even a cruise – or learned anything real that I cared about! Oh, damn. Why do some people have all the luck! Not that I mind typing – but it's always somebody else's things! Look at Aunt Edith, loving English literature, and grammar, and having dozens of girls adoring her that she can turn round her little finger! No wonder she stops short at the ankles."

A gull steered its effortless way across the field, it made a wonderful thing of its flight – trimming its weight to the light breeze. Hilda watched it tacking a few feet above her head; it flew so near that she caught a glimpse of its strange cold eyes. She found herself longing with a bitter longing to possess as cold and wild a heart.

Chapter 9

THERE was no good time for a talk until the evening. When Aunt Edith came back from Dover there was tea and supper to get, since it was Polly's evening out, and then Archer, the wire-haired terrier, had to be taken for his walk.

These were Aunt Edith's holidays; and they consisted very largely in fulfilling the expectations of Archer. In term time, Archer took second place; making what he could of a daily drive in Aunt Edith's car, and low life in between, with Polly. Archer disliked Polly, but he got a good deal out of her, one way or another. Archer was called after a gardener who had bestowed him as a pup upon Aunt Edith, out of gratitude for her development of his daughter's intellect. Aunt Edith was not only a good teacher, she was an uncommonly good teacher, and after she possessed him Archer's intellect had developed too, with the same rapidity as the gardener's daughter. He could beg, trust, die for his country, fetch and carry, and knew exactly when to obey and when to bully. In fact he was a Prestige dog; and had all the slightly flustered exactions and activities of a Prestige Person. He was quite willing to take any amount of trouble to be noticed, but he had to *be* noticed or he would not take any trouble at all, and Aunt Edith's holidays were rather too absorbed – even for a dog lover as Hilda was – in noticing Archer.

From first thing in the morning, when he scratched to go out, till last thing at night, when he scratched to come in – the day was punctuated with cries of "Where's Archer?" "Look at Archer!" "Has he hurt his paw?" "Have you seen his lead?" "Does he want a drink of water?" "Has Archer eaten his biscuit?" "Is that a strange dog coming?"

Walks were mere studies in Archer. It was useless to attempt a serious conversation, certain to be interrupted by Archer's pursuit of sheep, or by his dangerous approaches to the edges of cliffs; let alone the ever-present peril of Another Larger Dog. In a much lower, but longer category than his dangers, stood Archer's crimes. The things he must not do, and the things he wanted to do, had to be sorted out and separated without the slightest assistance from Archer. It was only when all these things were satisfactorily settled that Aunt Edith had any attention to spare. Even when supper was over, they had to play a game, which consisted in Archer wanting a stick when they had it, and *not* wanting it, when they did not. At last Aunt Edith said: "Archer had better go to bed, I think!" And Archer, having had a well-spent day with hardly a moment in which he had not been the centre of attention, curled himself round in a cushioned basket, and safely chased lions in his dreams.

It was a hot, slightly sticky August night. One of the nicest parts of Aunt Edith's bungalow was a little paved terrace outside the dining-room windows, facing the sea. The terrace was not very near the sea, for the sea was at the foot of the cliffs; and the edge of the cliffs was half a mile away. Still the air was full of the scent of brine, mingled with the penetrating sweetness of Aunt Edith's stocks.

The little pocket-handkerchief of a garden, through which Archer daily played the part of a West Indian hurricane, had still the remnants of a herbaceous border; and Hilda, leaning back in her steamer chair, could see the firm black heads of Oriental poppies, gently swaying in the moonlight.

Aunt Edith had been trying to talk about "groups" ever since she came back from Dover, and had been rather looking forward to consecutive speech upon the subject, as soon as Archer was safely off. She had got as far as, "In some ways I think they ought to be taken *seriously*, Hilda," when in the sudden flare of a match, she caught a glimpse of Hilda's face. In a flash she saw that Hilda had got to be taken more seriously than "groups." That stern, smouldering profile she had caught sight of, while lighting her cigarette, frightened Aunt Edith. She was used to young girls. She already knew that this favourite one – whom she always thought of as a thrown-away edition of herself – was in some kind of trouble, but until this moment she had no idea that Hilda's trouble was so dire.

During Hilda's last visit, Aunt Edith had been devoured by curiosity as to what was wrong with the girl, and had tried every method of extraction known to her; nor were there many such methods *unknown* to Aunt Edith; but she had always come up against a stone wall of silence. When Hilda had suddenly proposed this week-end visit, Aunt Edith had instantly asked herself, what had Hilda – without notice – come down for? It might have been most inconvenient! She might have had another guest! Polly might have gone on her yearly holiday! She might have let her bungalow! One does not expect even one's favourite niece without due notice, and Aunt Edith did not look upon a telegram sent the morning of the same day *as* due notice. On the other hand if Hilda was in any real trouble, if she wanted advice and assistance, Aunt Edith had been prepared to overlook it. She was quite willing to act as a mainstay to Hilda and to accept all the inconveniences of being a mainstay.

Aunt Edith despised her brother Tom, Hilda's father, for not having put his nose to the grindstone of education with the same ferocity as she herself; and even more she despised him for marrying Mary Catesby, the daughter of a tradesman in quite a small way, not to put too fine a point upon it – a greengrocer!

This damned him; and Hilda, poor child, was tarred with the same brush; but she had an intellect, and Aunt Edith had set herself to foster it, half out of natural affection, and half perhaps to spite Mary Catesby.

When Aunt Edith had received Hilda's telegram,

she had thought, with a spasm of eagerness, "Ah — now at last the poor child is going to confide in me!" and hastily added: "Perhaps I shall be *allowed* to help her," for Aunt Edith was getting slightly "group-ish," in spite of the reasons against it, but when she met Hilda at the station, she felt she had been mistaken, for Hilda no longer looked distraught and wild. She seemed curiously composed, as if the crisis — whatever it had been — was already over.

Still, Aunt Edith reflected, puffing thoughtfully at her cigarette, "Hilda is probably like me — not one of those people who *rush* for advice and help — but, having dealt with her crisis herself, she is prepared to discuss it afterwards in an intellectual way, with a fit person!"

Not advice, but reassurance was probably what Hilda wanted from her Aunt Edith, and though of course advice is more fun than reassurance, still to be a fit person is always something. Aunt Edith knew herself to be a superlatively fit person.

She was deeply experienced. She was fonder of Hilda than of any living being except herself and Archer; and what Aunt Edith did not know about other people's young men was hardly worth knowing.

This crisis of Hilda's, Aunt Edith swiftly decided, must be a young man crisis. Hilda was doing very well in her own little office; her health was unquestionable. She had no feeling for another woman greater than her affection for her Aunt Edith.

"And I," Aunt Edith virtuously reminded herself, "have always steered her clear of any sentimental attachment to me! She may idealize me – that can't be helped, with young girls and older women of the right sort – but there has never been any *inordinate* affection!" Aunt Edith was perfectly right about this; she was even more right than she would have cared to realize. A harsh, queer voice broke in upon Aunt Edith's reflections.

"Aunt Edith," Hilda said, "I've got something I'd like to talk to you about! Not groups!"

"Yes, it *must* be a young man," Aunt Edith told herself hastily; "not God – I think – she wouldn't sound *quite* so upset if it were God – at least not in *that* way!"

Aloud she said: "Yes, dear – I know!" in a voice that expressed the contented sympathy of omniscience.

It had never occurred to Aunt Edith that there were things that, as a woman, she *did not* know.

"You've heard of Ronnie," Hilda said doggedly, "the man we have as a paying guest. I've told you about him – haven't I?"

"Yes, dear," Aunt Edith said, although, as a matter of fact, all Hilda had told her about Ronnie was how much a week he paid, and that he was a medical student.

"I dare say you supposed I might get to like him," Hilda went on desperately. "It's the kind of thing people *do* suppose – and they have to be right sometimes – anyhow, I did! Not at once. At first I rather hated him! He knew such a lot. I didn't – and without meaning to – at least I think *then* it was without meaning to – he made me feel small.

"Anyhow, we used to have fights and arguments and things. He lent me books, and we talked politics for hours. He's not a Communist – and he's not exactly a Nazi. Still, I dare say if he had to choose, he might be a Nazi! Like all those capitalists, what they most want is to hold on to what they've got – nothing else really matters to them!"

"Possibly you're right," Aunt Edith murmured, "although you put it a little crudely!"

"Well, I *am* crude," admitted Hilda sombrely, "I always *was!* You know, Aunt Edith, sometimes I think being so much with you – and getting cleverer than the others – hasn't been awfully good for me! That sounds ungrateful – but I don't mean it ungratefully! I've loved all you taught me – but if you hadn't taught me, Ronnie would never have bothered about me! It's not as if I were pretty; what he liked me for *was* my wits. Besides, if he'd only wanted me as a lover, I'd have turned him straight down – because it wasn't what *I* wanted! But he liked talking to me – and I got – well, I got to care terribly for talking to him! He said that I had an intellect!"

"Well, darling, so you have," said Aunt Edith with real sympathy, for she could always be more sympathetic about intellects than about feelings; "and though it is quite true that you may have to suffer for your intellect, you will never be sorry, in the *end*, for having developed it! You can at least *understand* your own suffering! What has happened isn't the clumsy accident it might have been – if you hadn't wits! You remember that married man I told you about – Herbert – well, that *was* suffering, if you like – for both of us! But we sublimated it! as you will one day, I know, sublimate Ronnie!"

"Well, I may – but I doubt it!" Hilda said sombrely. "You see, we went a bit further than you did. He was my lover for a year!"

"Oh, Hilda!" Aunt Edith cried aghast. Her cigarette went out, and she felt cold – cold, and a little disappointed in Hilda; but then, she reminded herself, there was that Catesby element! You can't get rid of coarseness – not with a mother like Mary Catesby! Aunt Edith was surprised, and a little hurt; but she was not fundamentally shocked. She was an enlightened modern-minded woman, and after that one gasp of pained astonishment, she brought her emotions into line with her intellect.

"I do hope, my dear," she said with distaste, but without severity, "that at least you've avoided any danger of having a baby!"

"Yes. Ronnie knew all about that," Hilda said grimly. "He always knew how to avoid anything real happening! It isn't that that's bothering me! It's a funny thing, Aunt Edith, but in some ways I'd rather have *had* a baby! There would have been more *point* in going through all this – if there'd been something *alive* to show for it! Of course I quite see it would have been mad, from a practical point of view, and it wouldn't have made any difference to Ronnie – except that he'd have gone off into the blue – and left me to it! He hasn't gone away – yet. I've let him stay – there's the money, you see, and it doesn't make such a terrible difference whether he's there or not! I go out before he's up; and he's not often in before I'm in bed. I hardly ever see him. It's been finished since last holidays. He didn't care any more then; and now he hates me; and when he does see me, it's only to hurt me!

"He used to hurt me, even when he loved me – but I forgave him then – there was that difference. Now I don't forgive him!"

"Poor child!" Aunt Edith said softly. The whole thing, she told herself, might have been worse. Hilda had made a fool of herself, but not irretrievably. No one need know. Eggs have to be broken in order to make an omelet, but you need not leave the shells about. Hilda, her Aunt Edith realized, would be one of those who get rid of shells.

Hilda said nothing. She sat crouched and tense in her chair, leaning forward with her chin resting on her hand, gazing blindly into the garden.

She did not look as if she had quite finished her confidence, but neither did she look as if she wanted to go on.

Aunt Edith, of course, wanted to know more – much more. She wanted, in fact, to know everything. She waited for her sympathetic silence to tell; but the dark lump in the moonlight crouched rigidly still, and made no effort to seek further relief. "My poor child," Aunt Edith softly repeated. "Well, I am afraid such love affairs *do* end in just such a way! They haven't the *force* of the ideal to carry them on into victory – or to compensate them for defeat! Had Ronnie really loved you, he would, of course, have proposed a permanent union – not perhaps marriage, but not a hole-and-corner affair under your own roof; but you were not experienced enough to know this. You have had your lesson, and paid for it! I think you have shown a great deal of courage!"

It almost seemed as if Hilda did not care whether Aunt Edith thought she had shown a great deal of courage or not. She said after a pause, with a gesture of impatience: "He did propose a 'permanent union,' as you call it. He said he didn't believe in marriage till we could afford children – and anyhow, he thought, or *said* he thought, that love without marriage lasted longer. We were to have lived together, working independently at our own jobs, but sharing the same flat, directly he'd passed his finals. I suppose I ought to have known he didn't mean it, but I wanted to think he did."

"He has treated you very badly indeed!" Aunt Edith said, with a sudden sharp anger in her voice that surprised even herself. "Men have no right – no right at all – to – to take all that – on false pretences! Marriage is woman's chief safeguard, Hilda – never forget it. In fact, they haven't any other!"

"I dare say you're right," Hilda admitted rather wearily; "but you see, I wasn't thinking about safeguards. I was thinking about Ronnie."

"He should have thought of them – for you!" Aunt Edith said, the flame of her indignation rising still higher. "A *decent* man would have! Herbert . . ." She stopped abruptly. Herbert had wanted to go away with her for a week-end. It was Aunt Edith who, remembering the safeguard, hadn't gone.

"Well, I dare say Ronnie isn't decent," Hilda agreed listlessly, without noticing Aunt Edith's checked romance. "Certainly you couldn't call what he's doing now decent – he's making love to Annie!"

"What!" exclaimed Aunt Edith, now thoroughly roused. "Hilda, are you sure? What a – what an unmitigated *roué!* I never *heard* of such a thing! Twice – under the same roof! And of course your parents with their eyes glued together like dormice! Incredible conduct! That's what I call it – incredible!"

"The same roof," Hilda said with a queer little laugh, "doesn't seem to matter much – think of hotels!"

"Poor child!" Aunt Edith said to herself. "A coarsening experience! How wise I was to refuse!" Aloud she said, with some severity: "I hope that you have warned Annie."

"Yes – I've warned her!" Hilda answered bitterly. "And she – well, she thinks she's got more sense than I have – and perhaps she has! But, Aunt Edith, that's why I'm telling you – sense hasn't got anything to do with it. I know better than that anyhow. Ronnie will get his way by hook or by crook! And we've *got* to stop it! You and I – and I can't think how! I can't think how!"

These last words tore their way through Hilda's lips, and shook all the peace out of the moonlit garden.

They shook Aunt Edith. She sat quite still for a moment, not thinking about advice – just shaking.

Then she said, and reality had somehow or other crept from her shaking body into her words: "I will – I will try to help you, Hilda. I will indeed!"

"Then, that's all right," said Hilda; her voice was still hoarse, but that dreadful passion of fear and agony had gone out of it. She was trying now to be just the sort of courageous girl her Aunt Edith liked – not to make a fuss – not to upset an older person, whose feelings have ceased to react to acuteness – or to reciprocate it.

"You are quite *sure* your father and mother know nothing?" Aunt Edith asked briskly. This was a fact she wanted to get straight once and for all – her status in the matter depended upon it, and without status where – for some people – is the desire to help?

"I shouldn't suppose they did," Hilda replied cautiously. "Father certainly knows nothing – or he'd have blown the roof off! Mums you can't ever be quite so sure about . . ." Hilda paused, remembering a curious coincidence she had hitherto overlooked. Why had Mums never once suggested Hilda's carrying up Ronnie's breakfast to his room since their break? Up till then Hilda had always taken it, it was a practice she and Ronnie both prized; and yet she had never had to say to her mother that she was not going to do it! Automatically Mums had taken over the task; at exactly the right moment. "She can't know *much*," Hilda said at last, a little doubtfully. "Somehow she often seems to *understand* what she can't possibly *know!* Still, if she guessed what Ronnie was really like, she'd have hoofed him out of the house in a jiffy. She'd never have risked Annie! And she wouldn't know – as I do – and you too, I expect, Aunt Edith – that that would be the worst thing she *could* do! It would clinch Ronnie into getting complete hold of Annie, to pay us all out! And send Annie straight into his arms."

"Yes, I think you're right there," agreed Aunt Edith. "It's no use making people feel perverse to start with. I tell you what I really think, Hilda. I think I'd better see Ronnie myself! You see, up to now, he's never seen you in proper surroundings – and with a person of his own education. You've just been to him a girl in a class beneath him. Well, that makes an inferior person like Ronnie – for whatever class he belongs to, he has *behaved* like an inferior person – think he can do what he likes! He would never have dared to act with a girl he thought his social equal – as he has acted towards you! Well, bringing him down here *will* show him that you aren't really – or Annie either – quite so socially beneath him as he had imagined. I know you don't like admitting that your mother's birth *is* different – although in spite of Communism, which I haven't altogether accepted, I know it *is!* Still, don't you think yourself that we might try an appeal to Ronnie's honour – the appeal of an equal *to* an equal?"

Hilda hesitated. "Funny," she said at length, "if honour's anything, you'd suppose it 'ud go through everything – and that you'd even have it rather *more* for girls that are weaker, or poorer, or more handicapped socially than yourself – than for an equal! But I see what you mean right enough. Of course Ronnie *hasn't* any honour – but he'd like you to *think* he had!"

Aunt Edith got up decisively. "Stay where you are, Hilda dear," she said in her clearest and firmest tones. "I will go and ring Ronnie up! I shall ask him to come down to lunch here to-morrow, and meet him with the car – at Dover! I shall say that I believe we have something to talk over in a friendly way that had better *not* be put before your father and mother. He will see that, to avoid a row, he'd better come. Does he *like* avoiding rows?"

Hilda laughed again – that queer, grating laugh. "You may bet your bottom dollar he does!" she said. "He's never dared be alone with me once, since we broke! He locks his door in the daytime, if by any chance I'm in the house. He needn't! I'd rather touch hot iron than go near him! He knows all right what he's done, but sugar it over and he'll eat out of your hand. You're on the right track, Aunt Edith – you just let him know that he'll avoid a row by coming – and you'll get him! You can say I'll be out, if you like."

"Yes," Aunt Edith said reflectively, "I think that *would* be better, Hilda dear. You might take Archer with you, and have your lunch by the sea, but don't take him near the edge of the cliffs; and I'll give Ronnie lunch here. He can go back by the three-thirty – I'll run him to the station in my car – and be home in time for tea. Fortunately, to-morrow is Saturday."

Hilda laughed again, in fact as Aunt Edith turned swiftly through the French window, into the house, Hilda leaned forward, with her head in her arms, and shook with laughter.

Chapter 10

ON her way back to the hotel, after her last lecture, Dr. Silla felt very uneasy in her mind.

There was no ostensible reason for her dissatisfaction; since her lecture course was now over and had been an unqualified success. It was no light matter to give a course of lectures in a foreign tongue upon an abstruse subject; and Elena had not taken her task or its success lightly. Her future plans were made, and made in a way that should have increased her satisfaction. But she was very far from feeling satisfied. She dismissed an excited and friendly compatriot, from the door of her hotel in Tavistock Square, with an absent-minded kiss, although the compatriot had expected to come in. It was only eleven o'clock; and to a Czech mind the night was young. Fraulein Maria Schmidt had been looking forward to painting London a mild rose-colour with her famous friend. But she saw these expectations fade when she met the cloudy and aloof gaze that Elena bent upon her.

"I'm sorry, Maria," Elena said abruptly, "but I have something on my mind! To-morrow morning I will ring you up."

"But I shall come to see you off, of course. By the ten o'clock train from Victoria. It is all arranged, is it not?" Maria expostulated anxiously, for however famous one is, one has to catch boat-trains, since they do nothing whatever to catch celebrities.

"I will ring you up at eight o'clock to-morrow," Elena reflected in a tone that had the finality of a key turning in a lock. "Good night."

The hall of the hotel was dingy and empty, except for a white and puffy porter, who had just come in to take night duty. The porter was preparing to go to sleep in a cupboard under the stairs, in the clothes he stood up in, as a tribute to the idea of watchfulness.

Elena smiled as she passed him, and said "Good night" in such a friendly voice that he actually noticed her.

She then went straight upstairs, without bothering him to take her up in the lift to an extremely small and gloomy single room overlooking a water butt.

Elena clicked on the light, locked the door, and put her large hand-bag, containing passport, money, keys, and credentials, within reach of her hand during the night. She was afraid of nothing, but she took the precautions that people who are afraid sometimes forget to take.

As she undressed, she folded each garment quickly and with neat precision. She seldom bought clothes, but always looked as if what she wore were new. She washed herself briskly and thoroughly with lukewarm water, that was supposed to run hot; brushed her teeth, and then turned her attention with the utmost vigour to her thick block of red and glossy hair. When Elena had been young and mocked on her way to school because of it, the colour of her hair had stung her with acute shame; but she had learned to make a glory of it.

Once in bed, in a pair of striped blue and white pyjamas, Elena looked far more like a learned young man than a learned young woman. Her eyes and chin were those of a fighter; but of a fighter who usually fought with his wits.

"That girl," Elena said to herself, "hadn't of course posted my letter. Now *why* hadn't she? If she had merely forgotten to post it, why remember the lecture and take the trouble to go to it? She is not a careless girl – quite the contrary. She did not make slips, either in typing or in listening. If she were not sure of a word, she had the sense to stop and ask. She was not a flustered, cowardly girl, nor was she so vain that she had to show off – for in that case she would have typed before I was ready for her, and drowned my voice by her hurry – as most typists do; also she had a retentive memory and kept long clauses in her head without a perceptible effort. She looked ill and in distress, nevertheless she concentrated upon her task with an efficiency that proved that she was an exceptionally strong and able person.

"She gave me the impression also of being honest – as such persons usually are. But in the lecture hall she was ashamed to look me in the face. I think, if she had merely forgotten the letter, her conscience would have driven her to punish herself by confessing it. I waited an extra five minutes for her to do this – but she did not come! That girl is no coward, but she was doing something – in which the *not* posting of my letter played a part – something that was wrong and dangerous to do. It is a pity that psychology shows one a little, but seldom enough, of what other people are up to. Have I not always said 'Do everything oneself that may have disagreeable consequences if left undone' – and here I go, forgetting my own wisdom, and stepping into this puddle! Well, obviously I cannot leave London until I know for certain that they received or did *not* receive my letter at the Laboratory. But I will not ring up to-morrow morning to find out if I am expected, since I should perhaps get the girl into more trouble than her own.

"If they do not get the letter, it is most probable that they will ring *me* up to find out why I do not come. They have this address and telephone number. If by lunch-time they have not rung me up, I shall know definitely that they did not expect me and feel free to travel, and I shall distrust my psychology another time.

"In any event I must telegraph to Paris and postpone my journey. Also, to Cornelius, who will be enraged that I cannot meet him to-morrow, and I must telephone Maria to stop her going to the station.

"Two expensive telegrams and a telephone message. Also another night probably in this execrable hotel – where water to wash with is called hot and is tepid, and water to drink is called cold, and is also tepid. Their tea is good, but tea is a drink that should be taken as medicine, and their coffee, that should be used for pleasure, is wholly a punishment.

"I will therefore take tea for my breakfast to-morrow morning."

Dr. Elena Silla gave a long sigh, for she was a robust simple person, and enjoyed her pleasures in a whole-hearted fashion; still her sigh was not altogether for the missed coffee: She felt an unreasonable amount of pity for this girl who had caused her both expense and annoyance.

Next morning, when Elena had drunk her tea and sent her messages, she told the page-boy where she would be in case of a telephone call; and, not trusting him to remember, she took a draughty seat in a room miscalled a "lounge" where she could keep an eye on whatever took place in the hall.

She spent a long uncomfortable morning reading things she mortally disagreed with in the newspapers, and writing letters she had not intended to write; her handbag on her lap, and her luggage strapped and ready for departure. Perhaps with luck, she could get off to Paris by a later train on the same day, but it was raining heavily, and not the sort of day to expect luck.

At twelve-thirty there was a call for her, from a

Dr. Adrian Laing. Elena saw the page-boy looking about him in a dazed fashion, and hastened to his assistance. The voice at the end of the telephone sounded fierce from controlled agitation, it stated her name and repeated its own, but it did not ask her why she had not kept her appointment; instead it demanded, rather than asked, to be seen at once.

Dr. Silla replied, "Yes, I am free now. I should be indeed obliged if you would take a taxi and come here immediately, since I wish to leave London to-day."

The voice barked, "Yes! Yes!" and rang off.

"A young man in a hurry," Elena reflected. She had asked him no questions because she thought she would like to have a look at him first. "A nice voice, but badly rattled," she said to herself. "What *can* that girl have been up to?"

The bell-boy, slightly abashed by his omission to find Elena where she had told him to look for her, but encouraged by the direct and kindly smile she threw at him from the telephone box, quickly found her an empty room, where she could receive her visitor in peace with every prospect of privacy.

Half an hour later, Dr. Adrian Laing was announced. Dr. Elena Silla took people in steadily but slowly, and she had had hardly time to make up her mind about Dr. Laing, when he astonished her by glancing at her fiercely and exclaiming:

"But it isn't you!"

"Mad!" Elena said to herself, for even psychiatrists say "mad" when in a hurry rather than "mentally sick," "but they don't usually go mad in laboratories! Won't you sit down," she said aloud, reseating herself. "My name is Dr. Elena Silla and I assure you that I *am* myself!"

"Are you *really sure?*" this young man demanded with less anger and more uncertainty. "I mean—may I see your passport? And if you are – why didn't you come to the Laboratory this morning? And if you *didn't* come – who in God's name was the girl who *did?*"

Elena soothingly drew out her passport from the bag she was carrying and laid it on the table in front of him among her other papers. His agitated eyes roamed over an open letter *from* (not *to*) one of the heads of the profession; it began very warmly. Perhaps after all there *was* such a thing as a good Czech neurologist – whom Manning Foster ought to have known about – and if there was, this made it worse!

"Yes – I see – I see!" Adrian almost moaned, laying down the papers. "But you didn't! Somebody else came and gave your name – oh, damn! I mean – I'm sorry – I don't *want* to go to the police about her – but I suppose I shall have to!"

"Please sit down!" Elena repeated with inexorable firmness. He was such a tall young man, and he moved about so vehemently that the room seemed full of flying arms and legs and not at all conducive to reasoning. Adrian found his legs folding themselves up without his volition, and sat down.

"I think I may possibly be able to help you," Elena said in her low, musical voice, "if you would not mind, first, telling me exactly what happened this morning. After all, this affair has to do with me as well as with you, since the impostor used my name. I had not supposed there *were* any impostors among my acquaintances!" Elena gave a faint but friendly smile, and the young man began to pull himself together. She guessed that he was not a young man ordinarily in need of any such process. The eyes that met hers were a dark grey-blue; the lips were firm, and he held his head erect, without swagger or timidity. His glance was that of a man accustomed to observation, and to carrying out his observations with prompt decision. He was a personable young man, who had no habits of secrecy except those which he imagined were thrust upon him by his profession.

Elena felt that he was likeable and to be trusted, but she wondered a little why he was quite so much upset.

"This morning," he began, "at the hour of your appointment at the Lab., a young woman turned up, looking very much *like* you, but quite obviously *not* you. She gave your name. Naturally, *not* having heard from you to cancel your appointment, we were expecting you, and accepted her *as* you! Manning Foster had an important professional engagement, and being unable to be present, he had left me in charge. I was to show this lady – whom I supposed to be yourself – over the Laboratory. Half an hour after she had left – more by luck than anything else, I discovered that two tubes of a new Shiga bacillus were missing. I usually keep track of the tubes myself – in fact, of all the poisons – though it is actually the business of one of the Lab. boys. I sent for him, of course, and his reckoning agreed with mine.

"There can be no mistake about it – I only wish there could, but two of these highly lethal tubes *are* missing – and only missing since the girl was there. She *had* an opportunity to take them, for I left her for a few minutes at her request, to put in a long-distance call.

"You will understand that I thought it *was* you

who had taken them when I came here! I might almost say I *hoped* it was, since a foreign colleague might have taken such tubes from scientific acquisitiveness and without a criminal intent. There would be no danger to the public in this case – so I did not immediately ring up the police. *Now* I shall have to!"

"I'm rather glad you didn't," Elena remarked thoughtfully. "We may have to yet, but I think we may be able to get hold of the girl without! I happen to have at least an idea who she is. Yesterday I gave a red-haired typist (a stranger to me), whom I looked up in a directory, a letter to post to the Laboratory cancelling my appointment for this morning, as I found I must leave London by the ten o'clock train. I also gave this girl, who seemed an uncommonly intelligent and capable girl – at her own request – a ticket for my final lecture last night. She was there; I saw her in the audience; but she did not return my smile of recognition, she hung her head; and I gained the impression that she had forgotten to post the letter. To be on the safe side I therefore postponed my journey to Paris and awaited further developments. I thought if I failed to keep my appointment you would ring me up; if the letter *had* reached you nothing further need take place, and I was free to leave London by a later train. I am now very glad that I postponed my going. You thought the girl like me?"

The young man drew a deep breath of astonishment. "What an – I mean, did you really actually give up your plans on such a mere piece of guesswork?" he demanded.

"Guesswork?" Elena repeated stiffly. "I have no idea what you mean by such an expression! Is not 'to guess' in English to reach a conclusion without reasoning? I never make such wild jumps. I reason – and since what I reason upon are facts, I have an inclination to act upon my reasoning! You have not, however, answered my question – *was* this girl very like me?"

The young man's eyes changed – his whole face changed, and became younger and softer; his voice lost the rather dreary monotone of the English upper classes. "She was younger," he said gently, "perhaps six – perhaps ten years younger. Her face was very changeable – one couldn't be sure of her age! No, she wasn't *really* like you – your eyes haven't that hazel light – reddish-brown, you know, like bracken with the sun on it. Her mouth too was different! In repose her face was sad and – and sometimes almost angry; she was taller too, and er – er, she was a good deal slimmer; but she carried her head like you; and her hair was the same colour. I suppose if one had seen you before – at a distance – one might have mistaken you for each other!"

"Had you been to one of my lectures, perhaps," Elena said dryly, "and seen me with my hat off, she might not have taken you in."

The young man said quickly: "Yes, but of course I hadn't. None of us had!" and then coloured to the roots of his hair. Elena did nothing to help him out of this uncomfortable trap into which he had fallen; she merely smiled.

"A neurologist," she said indulgently, "who lectures on psychology, has no direct connection with such a Laboratory as yours. Pathological Laboratories overlook the human element. Otherwise you could perhaps have discovered that you were not showing round a colleague. Do you happen to know if this girl knew what the tubes contained?"

The young man dropped his eyes, and his hands twisted themselves on the arms of his chair, rather as if he were preparing to have a tooth taken out; then he looked up suddenly, and in his eyes shone such an essential humility that Dr. Silla, who had wanted to see if he possessed such a quality, felt instantly reassured. "I was a damned fool not to guess," he admitted. "Once I *did* think it was rather queer – what she said about an ordinary separator – but I don't know any Czechs! I thought they might be rather inaccurate and highfalutin as a race — if you'll excuse me — and I'm bound to admit that on the whole she took me in completely! You see, I wasn't expecting a lay person; I'm afraid I *did* tell her what was in the tubes!"

"Did you describe their lethal qualities?" Dr. Silla asked quietly.

"Probably I *did*," Adrian Laing admitted wretchedly. "I didn't *dwell* on them, of course — one doesn't look on poisons in that personal sort of way, does one, in a Lab.? They're just ingredients of one's work. I don't expect electricians keep thinking how many volts would do for a crowd! But I may have mentioned it — because, as a matter of fact, this particular bacillus *had* killed a whole family, and our culture was three times as strong as the original."

"It is unfortunate," Dr. Silla murmured, "that in the medical, as well as in other professions, we pigeonhole our knowledge! Well then, it is obvious that this girl took those tubes because she *knew* they contained poison. We shall have to get them from her as soon as possible, since presumably she intends to use them!"

"Must we — must we," Adrian stammered, "ring up the police?"

"It is your Laboratory! This is your country!" Elena Silla said sternly. "The responsibility is wholly yours. I can give you no advice whatever! I can, however, tell you one *fact* that may help you to a decision: It would be possible for me to act as quickly – and I hope as effectively – as the police. I could first find out where this girl lives, from her office boy, if she has already left the office; and when I have got the address I could call upon her.

"Further than this I can simply 'guess,' as I think you accused me once before of doing! And I 'guess' that she will not act *immediately* upon the possession of the poison. I am under the impression that she does not intend to commit suicide by poisoning. She would not, I think, take so much pains about throwing away her life, and like Queen Cleopatra, she would first find out if it hurt.

"At night, she has the River Thames at her disposal – by day, she would step off the curb under a motor-bus. I feel that she would take some active and desperate way, if she took any. But, to tell you the truth, the girl does not look to me like the type to which suicides belong."

"But – murder!" gasped the horrified young man. "You think that girl would – would *murder* someone? And so cruelly – so – so *inhumanly* cruelly?"

"She does not know, as you and I do, the exact symptoms of such a poison!" Elena told him. "Women have, as a rule, more pity than men, since they know more about pain – but nevertheless, they are the sex that most uses poison as a lethal weapon. Poison, you see, is sure, and needs neither force nor expert skill; and to most women, strength and expert knowledge are denied. After all, if you are intending to murder anyone it is presumable that you wish your act to be successful! But I do not think this girl is at all a murdering type. That is what makes her so interesting. She is merely headstrong – ignorant, and accustomed to take matters into her own hands; this implies that she will not hurry to use this poison, however great the incentive – for she probably intends to murder only as a last resort! Nevertheless we must run no risks. I will go immediately to find out her address and call upon her. Please let me have your number – at a place where I shall be sure to find you – until this evening. That is to say, if you have not decided to call up the police at once! Naturally, if you have so decided, I am equally at *their* disposal!"

"You don't suppose that she is – er – mentally deranged?" Adrian asked with an even greater humility. "I agree with you, she doesn't strike me as at all the murdering type – and I can't – I mean I hope –

it isn't suicide! But it might be a temporary fit of insanity, mightn't it?"

Elena Silla shook her head decisively. "That *not!*" she said, getting to her feet. "I do not mistake mental disorders. The girl is in a sharp state of conflict; and she is not acting with the balance of a normal person, but she is no more mad than you or I! She is desperately miserable, and also I should suppose very angry — and she has unfortunately an impatient disposition. These are, however, all states of mind quite common to the sane. She has not the cold logic of the insane. Now at what number shall I be sure to find you throughout the day?"

Adrian gave her a number, and said hesitatingly: "I might get a friend to take over for me, and leave the Lab. for an hour or two. I suppose I'd better not come with you?"

"Certainly *not*," said Dr. Silla with the utmost firmness. "By the by, have you told anyone else, at all, of these missing tubes? Will the Laboratory boy, for instance, report their loss to anyone in authority?"

"No!" Adrian answered promptly, but with the expression of a dog that has been refused a walk. "He's scared stiff anyhow! Besides I told him to hold his tongue. After all, I'm in charge of the Lab. and was, when she took it. The responsibility is therefore wholly mine. I shall keep it to myself till Manning Foster comes back from his golf this evening. He always looks in about nine, to see how things are going on. I suppose I shall have to report it then – unless you can tell me they've been destroyed. He won't miss them; unless it's brought to his notice, but I'd have to have your word for it!"

"You shall have the tubes themselves if I can get hold of them," Elena assured him, "only it may not be to-night. You see, it is very essential not to hurry her. Essential, I mean, for *her*. I promise no risks shall be run by the police, should we have to postpone getting hold of them."

"Then that's all right," Adrian said with obvious relief. "I leave it entirely to you, and I'm sure I can't thank you enough for helping us out like this!"

Elena concealed a smile. She had learned two things, by Adrian's explanations; one merely amused her – this was that Manning Foster had not thought enough of his foreign colleague to put off a game of golf to show her over his Laboratory; and the other, which she felt might be of definite use, was that the young man before her liked the girl he had seen at the Laboratory (impostor though she was) so much, that he had no intention of going to the police unless actually obliged to go to them.

"He must like her a good *deal*," Elena Silla said thoughtfully to herself, "since doctors are the last people in the world to condone murder! And as I think him to be a trustworthy human being himself, it is valuable evidence in favour of the girl. I, too, think she is a good girl, but I am less surprised than he is – at what a good girl may sometimes be tempted to do!"

Chapter 11

THE "staff" at Hilda's office displayed no reluctance in disgorging, for Dr. Silla, Hilda's home address. Harry, Hilda's shared office boy, was naturally disappointed to learn that no fatal accident had occurred to Hilda. If not a crime, an accident – and if an accident, fatal – was the way his dreams ran. Not that Harry had the slightest objection to the source of half his income – on the contrary, quite apart from the financial assistance he infinitely preferred Hilda as an employer to Miss Buckland. She was nearer the romantic age; and she was not without a human side to her. He had thought a good deal about Hilda's looks, and, had he put her into one of the sort of novels he habitually read, he would have called her "striking."

"Another red-headed one!" he thought regretfully, as Dr. Silla left him. "Now in a story, or a picture, that would have meant something! But you don't find the things that ought to happen on *these* stairs, believe me!" and he sighed heavily, and jerked his thumb in a rude way towards Miss Buckland's door, at a girl who had come to get her name put down at the registry office, and whom he thought, from her appearance, would not be likely to get a job very soon.

Rostrevor Road, when at last she found it, was rather a surprise to Dr. Silla. She had not expected anything beyond simplicity, but in Rostrevor Road simplicity had about it a strangely uninviting air. Each little house was so exactly like its neighbours, and each neighbour was so desperately depressing, that Elena could not help saying to herself with a sigh, "That poor smouldering girl – can one wonder she became fantastic!"

However, once inside the door of Number Twenty-four, Elena's impression of Hilda's circumstances improved. Mrs. Fenchurch was not a Catesby for nothing. Catesbys had all been workers, and worked hard; so that Mrs. Fenchurch had made a good thing of her job. Everything in the small house sparkled, from a superlative standard of cleanliness. The girls had seen to it that the walls were distempered a cheerful primrose, and had slowly weeded out the worst of their parents' furniture, replacing it – where it had to be replaced – with natural woods and pleasant colours.

There was no parlour, but a sitting-room where they all sat, with flowers and books in it – and a kitchen more charming still, which was used as a dining-room, and where Mrs. Fenchurch, although privately thinking copper pots old-fashioned, had polished them till they had the bright clarity of mirrors.

She herself had the kind of middle age that is no disgrace to any woman. She was plump but firm; always clean; and in the afternoons tidy.

"Fancy your coming all the way to get Hilda's address!" she said cordially, when she had discovered her visitor's errand. "That *is* a compliment, I must say, and she'll be sorry to miss you. Do sit down now, while I put the kettle on, and make you a cup of tea. I don't know when Hilda has missed a Friday afternoon at the office before. She's very faithful to her job, and no clock-watcher – that I will say for her, though I *am* her mother! To tell you the truth, it was *I* who persuaded her to take a long week-end off. She's not quite the thing – and a breath of the sea in September before you settle down for the winter is often just what'll put you right, isn't it? Hilda took her holiday early this year, and from what I can see, she didn't get much good from it! She won't *take* more than a fortnight, though she's her own boss!"

Dr. Silla sat down, and agreed to the cup of tea.

Mrs. Fenchurch was interested to learn that she was entertaining a doctor; not that she held with lady doctors, she was forced to admit. You had the sort of feeling that men *ought* to know better what they were about, even when they did not. Privately she thought that a lady doctor who lectured would be still worse.

Still this one seemed remarkably harmless and quiet; and had a reassuring likeness to Hilda.

Mrs. Fenchurch very seldom had the chance of a good talk with another woman who, while a good deal younger than herself, was considerably older than her daughter.

With neighbours, Mrs. Fenchurch never did more than pass the time of day. If she as much as mentioned that the man who sold fruit on a barrow was later than usual, it was quite as far as she thought it wise to go.

If you started being friendly with neighbours, they borrowed; or how did you know but they might turn out to keep opium dens?

"You find me quite alone this afternoon," Mrs. Fenchurch said, overlooking the fact that she was alone both mornings and afternoons as a rule, except Sundays. "My husband and my youngest girl Annie never come back from their business until six o'clock; and our young lodger, who is a medical student, may just run in for a cup of tea, before he's off motoring for the week-end – or he may not! We got into the habit of letting Annie's room while she was abroad for a year – something the matter with her lung she had – an apex, I think the doctor called it, but I'm glad to say whatever it was, she seems to have left it behind her in Switzerland! And that extra thirty shillings a week from letting the room is a big help, so the girls decided to share. Sometimes our young fellow is a bit late with his money. Still he's a real gentleman and all of us fond of him, and that's everything, isn't it? I wouldn't have anyone in the house that hadn't nice ways with him – pay what he might!"

"We also sometimes take paying guests in my home," Elena reassuringly told her. "It is a good way of using extra rooms, I think, and you have made this home so pretty, that it must be easy to get a good visitor."

Privately Dr. Silla was thinking: "She talks, this woman, because she is lonely! I do not think she would make a bad mother. I doubt if she would either pamper or bully a child. Hilda's temper must have come from a different cause! Perhaps envy of the younger girl?"

"And your other daughter," she asked after a pause, "has she your daughter Hilda's good looks also?"

"My Annie," Mrs. Fenchurch said with pride, "without my calling her a beauty, is as pretty a girl as you'll find in *this* street, or many another! And what's more, what you don't often find with pretty girls – she's liked with it!

"You wouldn't believe the inquiries that were made about her, while she was away, or the fuss her friends made of her when she came back! Quite like royalty, I used to say to my husband. Hilda – well, Hilda's different. She's always been one to hold herself aloof – and cleverer no doubt than anyone, except Ronnie, that she'd be at all likely to meet! But whatever other people think of her – from the outside, as it were – she's worth her weight in gold to her mother. What I say is, they may be in the way or they may not, but you can't help having brains if you've got them, whether other people like them or not, can you?"

Dr. Silla smiled sympathetically. "At any rate," she

said, "having someone in her own home, who can share her intellectual interest, must have been good for your eldest daughter?"

"Ah!" said Mrs. Fenchurch, with a long sharp sigh, and her expression changed into one of bewildered regret. There was a long pause, which Dr. Silla did nothing to break; she simply went on looking sympathetic. "Well, of course, in a sense," Mrs. Fenchurch began with another, but less mysterious, sigh, "Ronnie might have been a help. But in another sense I don't think he *has* been. I'm sure I don't know why I go on talking to you like this, but I haven't anyone else I *can* talk to – and I'm downright worried, and that's a fact!" Mrs. Fenchurch still hesitated – here was her opportunity and perhaps she would never get such another. This woman was not only another woman of greater experience and more training than herself, but she was also a stranger, and could be counted upon – since she was a foreigner into the bargain – to remain a stranger!

Dr. Silla said the one thing that Mrs. Fenchurch could never resist, and, as it was a fact, it carried with it a sense of conviction. "I like your daughter Hilda," she said quietly, and needed to say no more.

"Well," Mrs. Fenchurch went on, in a rush, "when Ronnie first came, it *did* brighten Hilda up. It brightened her up wonderfully. There they were at it, hammer and tongs, discussing anything and everything, and friendly with it! I'd never heard Hilda talk that way before. I hadn't thought she *could!* and they went out together in the evenings. Mr. Fenchurch commented on it sometimes, but what I say is, you've got to let young people take their own way, they do it anyhow – whether you let them or not! But after a time, it sort of wore off! And then when Annie came home – Well, I'd have thought nothing of it, if the *three* of them had gone out together in the evenings, or if Ronnie had taken them by turns sometimes! I'd have been contented with *that*. But it sort of dropped altogether, if you know what I mean, and I admit to you, Dr. Silla, I didn't like it at all! You can't say it's Ronnie's fault exactly, if he likes one rather than the other – especially as, between ourselves, I don't expect he takes either of them very seriously. Flying higher, in the long run, I should expect. And I've hinted it once or twice to both of them, though naturally at their age they don't agree with me. They're always talking of a classless world, both of them, and perhaps it would be all very well in its way, but we haven't got there yet! That's what I tell them, and though I'm fond as fond of Ronnie – he treats me like his mother, and I *feel* like that *to* him – he's not the boy that would put up with anything he thought was a second best – if there *was* a first!"

"Ah!" murmured Dr. Silla, as if she already saw what kind of boy Ronnie was. "And perhaps this is Ronnie coming in now?"

The gate banged, the door flew open, and Ronnie stood on the threshold, for a flying second undecided which role to play. It was, Elena Silla thought, watching him, like fixing a chameleon the moment before it changes colour. "I can better understand murdering him than loving him – " passed through Elena's mind, and yet this uncomplimentary sentence was strange, for Ronnie continued – even in his moment of indecision – to look exceedingly attractive. A little diffident, a little surprised, a little uncertain how *much* at home it would be worth his while to make himself – these quiverings of instinct passed over him as lightly as a breeze ruffles the surface of a lake – leaving it satin-smooth again the moment after.

Should he get his tea, as he had intended, risking being bored by this strange red-haired woman, who did not look like a district visitor and yet could scarcely be anything else; or should he miss an uncommonly good tea, and dash off with his suit-case, for his week-end visit?

Deciding that as, in order to get off early, he *had* already missed his lunch, he really could *not* miss his tea, Ronnie's face lit into sudden radiance. Dr. Elena Silla, still regarding him with her clear, effortless eyes, thought that she had never seen such a terrific concentration of charm in any one person before.

It was as if Ronnie generated electricity on the premises, to supply himself with light.

"What a lot," she said to herself, while Mrs. Fenchurch made an explanatory introduction, "*someone* must have to pay for the upkeep of all that charm! And how tired the poor boy himself must get working it all up!" That was probably the trouble; Hilda had had to pay for Ronnie's charm; and the moment had arrived when she had had to pay too much. All the exhaustion, irritation, malice, envy, and worry so highly trained an effort must involve, in the soul of the artist creating it, had no doubt been worked off on Hilda.

Hilda looked like that – she looked like someone who has for a very long time taken kicks – first as *well,* and then *instead* of ha'pence. Her emotions had been so switch-backed between agony and ecstasy that she had lost her sense of balance.

"This is the murderee!" Elena thought with a faint smile of amusement. "Well, in my opinion, poor weak boy, he is hardly worth a crime – and certainly *not* worth making oneself into a criminal *for!* I am surprised at Hilda!" Dr. Silla sat up a little straighter, for this was the effect that Ronnie had upon her, and began to add up, in her mind, the sum of Hilda's difficulties. Typing – a wearying profession for a creative mind! Rostrevor Road – an exasperating background! Mrs. Fenchurch – not a definite hindrance, but perhaps indefinitely a provocation – because uneducated, and because loved.

Annie – a very difficult bone in the throat for an elder sister to swallow! Delicate – pretty – abroad – beloved! It would not have been easy for anyone to make a good thing out of such disadvantageous comparisons. An irritable father! And last, but not least, Ronnie as a lover! and almost certainly a *first* lover!

Once more Dr. Silla glanced at Ronnie. He really had not good looks; and yet with his consummate cleverness, he had managed to make that long, whitish, weak-mouthed face rather attractive. His eyes – muddy when in repose – were now swimming in a sort of golden light. His hair, a dull brown, but worn a trifle long and waved, as Dr. Silla unkindly thought, artificially, was becoming to him. "He *arranges* his face well!" she told herself, "but he can't *quite* manage those thin sadistic lips. They're definitely helpless, and therefore cruel! Poor creature! Cruel to anyone who loves him – and cruelest of all to the one who loves him most – and who will always love him most – himself! It could only have been the fact that Hilda was dull and lonely – and no doubt had no sex life at all at twenty-five – that made her turn this very light-shaped love affair into so great a tragedy!"

"Forgive my saying so," Ronnie remarked, swaying towards Dr. Silla in a manner that he contrived to make intimate without impertinence, "but you're awfully like 'our' Hilda! Isn't she, Mums?"

How delicately he contrived to make it plain that he knew the Fenchurches were common! With what courtesy and tenderness even he brushed in, with his light touch, the exact shade of their inferiority – to Dr. Silla and himself! Could she appreciate the lovely tact of his warm but intelligent heart? Apparently Dr. Silla *was* able to appreciate it, for she smiled, and when she smiled all the heaviness went out of her face, and Ronnie saw that she had been worth pleasing.

"I know that I am like Miss Fenchurch," she admitted slowly, in her strange deep voice, "though I am indeed flattered by such a comparison – for she is much younger and better-looking than I! Perhaps you will be seeing her this week-end, for I hear you are also going away? If so, I should be grateful if you could give her a message from me, that I have some typing for her to do."

The young man's face fell, so that Elena knew he did not like – and would not have liked – the prospect of meeting Hilda over the week-end – and then it fell still further, with an artificial gloom, to prove how sorry he was, not to be able to serve Elena.

"*So* sorry," he said with emphasis, "I should so much have liked to take any message for you, but I'm sure *not* to see her." He was quite certain of that, and could, Dr. Silla thought, be trusted to carry this certainty out.

Well, that was all right – then he could not be murdered by Hilda over the week-end! It was all that Elena really wanted – now that she had seen him – to know from Ronnie.

She rose to her feet, thanked Mrs. Fenchurch with cordiality for her kind welcome, and took Hilda's present address, so that she might write for an appointment on Monday.

It all went very easily. Ronnie, though really anxious, now that he felt he had impressed her agreeably, to have Dr. Silla stay – dashed to the door with her, and gave her the fullest possible directions, as to how to get away from Rostrevor Road. His eyes were full of a curiosity he rather hoped she would take this occasion to satisfy, but Dr. Silla had had enough of Ronnie.

She thanked him rather less lingeringly than he expected, leaving him, in fact, still saying something charming, which she did not take the trouble to catch. Paying no attention at all to his skilled directions, she looked for, and after a time found, a public telephone.

"It's all right," she told the eager ear of Adrian Laing. "She won't do anything over the week-end. Shall I return the tubes, or destroy them – when I've got hold of them?"

"Better return them," Adrian advised. "It might make a shindy, if it turned out that they were missing! I'll soothe the Lab. boy's mind – and I needn't say I'm both infinitely relieved and infinitely grateful to you, into the bargain! Only – only couldn't you tell me a little more about it? How you managed, and so on – I mean – One can't help being interested, can one, in the human side of it?"

"Certainly, I will tell you everything when it *is* all settled," agreed Dr. Silla, smiling broadly into the inanimate mouthpiece of the telephone. "And to go on with, although there *is* never sufficient reason for a wrong act – there were, in this case, many excuses. She wished, in particular, to save a little sister from a bad affair! But there was no need, of course, for such a strong measure – the little sister can, I feel sure, be saved without!"

She heard a long sigh of relief, then Adrian said a little stiffly, almost as if he could see her smile:

"Naturally one's relieved. She did not look like a criminal type!"

"Types – these I do not greatly believe in," Dr. Silla replied. "Each person is different, and they behave as they think that they wish to behave! But not as they wish to *think* that they behave! In particular, this is a good girl, but we shall need to prove it to her – and for this I may need your help!"

There was a pause before Adrian answered with an eagerness he thought he had concealed by his delay in answering: "In what way could I be of any help?"

"I don't know myself yet," Dr. Silla admitted, "but if you would keep yourself free over the weekend, I should be glad to be able to ring you up!"

"Yes – I could do that!" Adrian agreed with promptitude; and he was going to ask a further question, but found that Dr. Silla had already rung off.

Chapter 12

THE VOICE at the end of the telephone was dulcet, but it held a tincture of iron. Ronnie was an expert in the tones of human voices, especially those of women; and he recognized that this was a woman who meant to get her own way, and who would cut up rough, perhaps even dangerously rough, if she didn't get it.

It was also obvious that she knew a good deal, if not all, about his cursed affair with Hilda; and that what she knew of it, she did not like.

Hilda was staying with her; but he needn't see Hilda – that was something. The person he would have to settle with was Miss Fenchurch, Hilda's schoolteacher aunt.

"We must either talk it over by ourselves, *here*,"

the voice had said, very distinctly for a long-distance call, "or I shall be obliged to come up to town, and see Mr. and Mrs. Fenchurch."

Almost anything was better than that! An aunt one might be able to turn; but immediate families always take sides with their own members.

If beans were to be spilled – let them at least be spilled at a distance from the place where Ronnie actually lived.

Besides, there was Annie! Ronnie's hazel eyes, attractively large and clear, gazed with unusual fixity at the telephone receiver, which he held delicately away from his mouth, for fear of catching something.

Why should he be forced to put a chill into that warm, happy, fluid relationship with little Annie? Why should it so soon be made to jell, robbed at one and the same time of its fluidity, and of its happiness?

Surely there could be no need for any such drastic measure, just because of Hilda?

Ronnie cleared his throat in a light baritone way, and accepted Miss Fenchurch's kind invitation to lunch with her the next day at Dover.

He was in fact staying with friends in the neighbourhood, and nothing could be easier; but it would be as well perhaps for him not to meet Hilda, since there was a little misunderstanding between them, that had not yet been cleared up.

Miss Fenchurch's voice was still dulcet, but the flavour of iron had increased. "My niece would prefer *not* to meet you at present," she told Ronnie, as if Hilda's preferences were the ones to be attended to, "and I shall expect you at one o'clock," and before Ronnie had time to renew his thanks, she had hung up the receiver.

It was a public telephone box, and Ronnie was quite glad to get out of it. He had a conscience that only felt sore when he was left alone with it, but even then he could do a good deal to relieve its ache. One need not dread exposure, Ronnie reminded himself, so long as one is allowed to be the showman of the exposed object.

How many people who might perhaps have thought unkindly of Ronnie, now, after his explanations, thought unkindly of somebody else?

Surely all his friends could not be deceived in him? So many – and such good, dear helpful people – *must* be right?

When Ronnie felt himself actually threatened, and had time to work himself up, he could always succeed in ridding himself of any sense of guilt. He saw himself like the Saint Michael in Correggio's glowing masterpiece, lightly decked with blue ribbons, stamping upon a rather trifling lizard, already under his feet. Hilda in this case was the lizard.

Saturday was a fine day; and Ronnie's "Star" lent him her own two-seater, and saw him off, with cheering laughter, from her garden gate.

"Honeymead," Aunt Edith's house, stood on a square of imported gravel, flanked by two bungalows as irrelevant as itself. They spoiled the clean run of the green cliff's edge, above its shining white precipice; but inside Aunt Edith's rooms were open, airy and sophisticated.

Aunt Edith was not yet forty. She had the erect, slightly rigid figure often to be found in those who impart instruction to the young. She must have been quite pretty ten years ago; and very pretty indeed fifteen years ago.

Her features were good, but faintly nipped, as if she had been sent to a dry cleaner's once too often. Her colouring was clear, but not glowing; every hair was in place, none was grey; and she wore spectacles.

She gave Ronnie an extremely good lunch – cold, but it was a hot day; salmon, with a mayonnaise sauce reminded Ronnie rather pleasantly of Hilda, and went very well indeed with Devon cider.

A little breeze stole in between orange curtains; and there were marigolds that Archer had not yet dug up, just outside the window.

They discussed the boat race, Aldous Huxley's pacifist opinions, and Greta Garbo.

Aunt Edith wanted to know, over the coffee, what Ronnie thought of groupists.

Ronnie told her, very amusingly and at some length. He had no use for groupists; but Aunt Edith remained tolerant and not so sure.

They went into a still nicer room for their coffee – with big bow windows, and nothing between them and the invisible sea.

Aunt Edith gave Ronnie a cigarette; and he lit first hers, and then his own, with an increasing sense of ease, and even mastery; but a slight frostiness was once more noticeable in Aunt Edith's manner.

"We must," she said quietly but firmly, "have this thing out, Mr. Marsh – man to man! You know what I am talking about of course – this unfortunate affair with Hilda – and perhaps not only with Hilda! I understand there is some question of Annie as well! I must say that this adds very seriously to the unpleasantness all round! A love affair is a thing that may happen to anyone – even though, of course, such a one as yours with Hilda is distressingly out of place in the *home* – if you will forgive my saying so – of a young and innocent girl; but when it occurs to a second one under the same roof – well – one need not be considered old-fashioned or strait-laced if one *is* rather horrified to hear of it!"

Ronnie looked thoughtfully at Aunt Edith. The worst of young middle-aged women, when they are unmarried, is that they may equally well belong to the kind that cherishes extreme innocence and likes to be thought pure as lilies; or the other kind that wishes to be thought extremely rakish, or at any rate tolerantly knowing of the rakishness of others. Now to which category did Aunt Edith belong?

He leaned back in Aunt Edith's most comfortable armchair, and shook his long crossed leg thoughtfully but not impatiently; it seemed rather to move as the stem of a water-lily might move, to the soft swell of a current far beneath the surface.

"I dare say it looks like that," Ronnie said after a long pause, which he utilized by shifting his cigarette ash onto a scarlet saucer, set conveniently at his elbow, and quite probably coming from Japan.

"But you and I know very well, Miss Fenchurch, how extraordinarily different real love affairs are from what one or the other of the disillusioned pair tells you, when it is over! Hilda, poor child, knows that whatever was between us *is* over; and as she was – if I may say so without caddishness – the hardest hit, I'm sorry to say she feels the most injured. But if I'm to be perfectly honest with you – as I already see that I *can* be – neither of us has very much to be injured about. We thought we cared for each other, and we tried to make a go of it – and failed. We both believed – as I still believe – in trial trips. Well, the trial proved to us that we didn't fit.

"Hilda minded, and I didn't, at least not so much! Now, Miss Fenchurch, you're a woman of the world, and you probably know that the person who kicks up the most dust isn't, by any means, always the most innocent. I'm going to throw myself on your intellectual mercy – and leave a good deal to it, that I frankly can't explain. I don't want to complain of Hilda, but girls aren't always quite what their aunts think, are they? Especially not such an aunt as I see you are. I don't want to flatter you, but I *do* know an immaculate woman when I see one! I assure you, you would be the last person in the world before whom Hilda would show her natural tendencies!" Ronnie gave Aunt Edith a slow reverent look that was exceedingly effective. He had decided that Aunt Edith was the kind of woman who would like to have it both ways, so he was giving it to her both ways: the lily-white stunt combined with the-wisdom-of-the-serpent; and Ronnie could see by Aunt Edith's face that she was taking the mixture remarkably well.

"I don't mean that I think that Hilda is in the least vicious," Ronnie went on after a slight pause. "She is merely passionate; but a passionate girl who takes a fancy to you – innocent or not innocent – is no joke to live with under the same roof! I don't want to put too fine a point upon it, but I shouldn't advise even a Galahad to try it. After all, virginity isn't purely technical, is it? There's a virginity of the mind . . . Well, Hilda hasn't got that – and what's more, she never had! Perhaps that is where the Catesby element comes in! You'll forgive my saying so, but there isn't much doubt that your brother married beneath him."

Aunt Edith more than forgave Ronnie for this statement. She enjoyed it to the roots of her being.

"Yes, indeed," she said with a long regretful sigh, "my brother made a cruel mistake – for all of us – as well as for himself! Poor child – poor Hilda! I see what you mean!"

"Very well then," Ronnie went on, his grave eyes resting upon Aunt Edith's face, with the effect of complete and touching frankness. "Now I've said all

I've got to say – all I *can* say about Hilda and myself; and we'll go on to Annie. Annie is a dear little thing!" Ronnie paused for a moment, remembering an appropriate phrase that had occurred to him once before in dealing with the subject of Annie. "She's like a speedwell in a country lane – exquisitely pretty, and just as common."

Aunt Edith sighed deeply. "How true," she observed, and Ronnie saw that in this brief phrase Aunt Edith's family colours had fallen from the mast. "How true *that* is! My poor brother!"

"I should never dream," Ronnie went on, ignoring this revealing interruption, and allowing himself to show emotion for the first time, though of an austere, an almost disapproving kind, "I should never dream of taking Annie seriously, far less of asking her to take *me* seriously! I don't deny that I have shown her a flirtatious interest – which is what she asks, and gives every man she meets. But I do assure you most earnestly, Miss Fenchurch, that this is all there ever was, or ever will be, in this affair – if you can even *call* it an affair – between Annie and me! Hilda and I were definitely a serious proposition, but with Annie and myself everything is as light and passing as a soufflé omelette."

"Still it *is* under the same roof," Aunt Edith a little shamefacedly suggested. "One can't *quite* get away from that, can one?"

Ronnie had, as a matter of fact, got clean away from it; and he knew that Aunt Edith was by now eating out of his hand, so that a little thing like a roof wasn't going to divide them for long.

There is always a moment, between a man and a woman, when the moral sovereignty passes from one to the other. This moment had taken place when Aunt Edith had said, "How true *that* is!" Ronnie was to be the Leader from this time forward. Still he didn't rub his moral leadership in; instead, he gave her his most winning smile, – a straight, confidential, man-to-man smile, – and slightly shrugged his shoulders. "I could leave to-morrow," he reminded her; "but there is the question of the family exchequer. I do the best I can for that, Miss Fenchurch. Your brother isn't very well off, you know, and his wife does rather, I'm afraid, depend on me for the little extras that make all the difference in the housekeeping – I should hate it if she came down on you instead!"

This was less clever of Ronnie, for Aunt Edith was both generous and proud. She stiffened again slightly, and said in rather a dry voice: "My sister-in-law has never borrowed from me in her life, though I should be delighted to lend her anything if she wanted it."

Ronnie apologized. "One only knows what *can* happen," he explained, "and I always think it such a shame when it *does*. Ties of blood – especially between mixed social classes – can be the very devil!"

Aunt Edith's stiffness melted.

The whole horizon had somehow or other changed. Hilda, from darkening the sky, had become a cloud as small as a man's hand.

The talk veered to girls in general, and they talked objectively and animatedly about girls, for over an hour.

Aunt Edith knew a great deal more about this subject than Ronnie did, or indeed ever would know; but she did not know quite the same things as Ronnie. Their standards of comparison were different. Flirts, for instance, were a sealed book to Aunt Edith, and no girl in her senses would have unsealed it.

Aunt Edith had a vague, fastidious idea that flirts were almost the same as housemaids. She never heard the word "flirt" without envisaging a butcher boy at the corner, and the sound of osculation at dusk close to the back door.

She had herself been brought up purely academically and almost without a male acquaintance.

Those she might have had were at the War, or in training for it; and not very many of them came back.

Aunt Edith had gone to college; and loved Newnham instead.

Later on, a very great deal later on, had occurred the incident of the married man. It had been very serious indeed to Aunt Edith, so serious that she intended it to do for the rest of her life.

She was therefore quite unconscious that Ronnie was flirting with her now; and perhaps even further from the seat of her consciousness was the knowledge that she was enjoying it.

Presumably they were both enjoying it, just because it meant so little to either of them. It was an ideal way of spending a summer afternoon.

Aunt Edith became more and more sure that Ronnie was a most delightful young man, who had been led into a most unfortunate episode through Hilda's excitable passions, for which he was in no way responsible, while his intentions towards Annie were so honourable as to be non-existent.

Aunt Edith couldn't help realizing that had she

been ten years younger, or Ronnie ten years older, they might very well have "fitted in," as Ronnie so charmingly called it, far more satisfactorily than Ronnie could ever have fitted either of her nieces. Wisdom was Aunt Edith's strong suit, and she played it for all she was worth, while Ronnie idly wriggled his long leg, and smoked cigarette after cigarette, enjoying the fresh sea air, and the sound of a voice almost as "Oxford" as his own.

In fact so comfortable and successful did Ronnie feel that he would gladly have stayed on till tea, had he not been afraid that Hilda might, at any moment, plunge in, with her usual bumble-puppy activities.

She ought of course to be delighted at seeing him getting on so well with her aunt, since it had been — while their own affair was on — her fondest dream. But Ronnie had, in those days, avoided the opportunity. He knew what a bore aunts could be, especially learned ones. It would be illogical of Hilda, however, to mind his doing what she had once incited him to do. "Make friends with Aunt Edith," she had unduly often pleaded; but now she would, metaphorically speaking, want to scratch his eyes out for doing it.

Ronnie wisely believed in keeping all his intimacies separate. Like Saint Paul, he tried to be all things to all men — but, probably unlike Saint Paul, the things Ronnie tried to be were all different things. You cannot be a roistering blade with a Plymouth Brother, for instance. Saint Paul might have made this mistake, but not Ronnie!

Ronnie reminded Aunt Edith regretfully that he had to get back to his friends; and Aunt Edith remembered that she had a tea engagement she would have gladly postponed.

Ronnie asked wistfully if they might not someday meet again; and Aunt Edith was very gracious about it, and even accompanied him to the garden gate.

Ronnie held her hand, rather longer than he should have done at parting; and Aunt Edith let him hold it.

She went back into the house again, feeling very pleased with Ronnie, still more pleased with herself, and a very great deal less sorry for Hilda.

"If girls *will* flirt," she said severely to her own rejuvenated image in the glass, giving herself a slightly accentuated touch of lipstick, "it can't of course be helped — but they should, at least, be prepared to face the consequences!"

Chapter 13

IF IT had not been for Archer, Hilda would have concealed herself in the bungalow until she heard the sound of Ronnie's voice.

For the sound of Ronnie's voice still retained its power to charm her. His face no longer lit her heart — his actual words filled her with anger or shame; but she could not hear the sound of Ronnie's voice without a wave of uncontrollable joy flooding her whole consciousness. Like the lover in Tennyson's "Maud," she knew that her

> *"Dust would hear it, and beat,*
> *Had she lain for a century dead."*

It was nonsense, of course, she told herself, for Ronnie had not even a beautiful voice. He spoke with the clipped tonelessness of the English upper classes, always stingy of emotion, and determined to keep what little they had, private.

Still she could not get over it; when Ronnie said: "Hilda!" it made her name so precious that she used to wince when other people used it too soon afterwards.

It was no use waiting to hear Ronnie's voice now, for Archer would certainly bark, and then Aunt Edith would give the show away, by wanting to know whether Hilda had gone off, without him. If Ronnie caught the barest glimpse of Hilda, Aunt Edith's pitch would be queered, and the whole interview rendered useless.

To avoid temptation, therefore, Hilda, accompanied by the bounding, barking Archer, dashed out of the bungalow long before Ronnie was due to arrive. She had a curious moment first, while she was helping Aunt Edith prepare a specially delectable lunch. Polly, the girl, was out for the whole day. Aunt Edith had just finished a fish salad, and asked Hilda, who was an adept at mayonnaise, to make the sauce, while she changed her dress.

Aunt Edith did not eat mayonnaise; she served it separately in a sauce-boat; and Hilda knew that Ronnie was particularly fond of it.

It would not have taken her a moment to run upstairs and get one of the tubes, and conceal it in the beaten eggs. But she dared not risk it. Supposing, only supposing, that someone else dropped in who *did* like mayonnaise, or that Aunt Edith, who had a weathercock mind, changed it? Suppose Aunt Edith said: "Now, after all *do* I hate mayonnaise as much as I think I do? Let me be brave and see! I always believe in constant experiments!"

If it served her purpose to find that she *had* changed her taste, Aunt Edith might swallow half the sauceboat. No, it was safer to wait till Hilda was at home, and could prepare a meal solely for Ronnie; and see it safely carried upstairs into his room by Mums. No one else would touch anything on Ronnie's tray — not even Annie.

Hilda felt greatly relieved when she stood on the cliff's edge, with Archer chasing gulls, and remembered that the contents of the tube were *not* in the mayonnaise. The air sparkled; the turf ran smooth under her feet; beneath the shining chalk precipices, the grey-blue sea splashed softly. The small summer waves hardly broke the edge of the sea's silvery, satin surface.

Archer found himself unaccountably free. No voice warned him to beware of cliffs, to spare sheep, to avoid doubtful encounters with other dogs. He could roam – he could be lawless – he could run risks; but he could not, while doing these things, arouse notice; so that after a time these pastimes palled, and Archer did what he'd never been known to do when supplicated – he kept close to heel.

Even this glittering conduct failed to attract Hilda's attention; her mind was absorbed over Aunt Edith's interview with Ronnie. It raced with cruel speed, turning this way and that, but no longer inventing a desired solution. Hilda could not contrive to make the scene come her own way, because she *had* now no way, that led back to Ronnie!

All ways led away from him.

Still some were easier to follow than others – a road that led Ronnie away from Annie was the easiest. But *would* Ronnie give Annie up? He might *say* he would, to Aunt Edith; he might – led by the swift responsiveness of his easily aroused emotions – believe for a moment that he *could;* but as soon as he left Aunt Edith's potent presence, would not the fragile edifice of his chivalry begin to crumble?

Ronnie always loved to be a hero, till he reached the point of giving up what he wanted, and then he would see some other way of being a hero *without* giving up what he wanted!

He would write Aunt Edith a wonderful letter, to make her think this new way was "a far far better thing" than what he had promised to do – while all the while it was the exact opposite – merely the dog returning to its vomit – with a gift for language to conceal what he was up to!

The lonely day burned serenely on; but Hilda's eyes did not see the golden fields they looked on. Her ears did not hear the eager thrilling of the larks' songs, nor the light laughter of the breaking waves. Hilda came to a knowledge of the other world only when she all but fell over a lady sitting against a low bank, eating sandwiches.

Then indeed Hilda's consciousness roused itself with a vengeance, for the lady was Dr. Silla, who ought to have been, by this time, safely on her way back to Czechoslovakia.

Hilda stopped dead – for one wild moment it occurred to her that she was suffering from an hallucination. An experience common, she believed, to murderers – but surely not common *before* the murder has taken place?

But when Dr. Silla smiled, Hilda knew that this was no hallucination. There was something singularly real about Dr. Silla's infrequent smiles.

"But you – you oughtn't to be here!" Hilda gasped. "Weren't you leaving England yesterday morning?" And then as panic clutched at her very heart-strings: "Have you *been* to the Laboratory, after all?"

"I had written to tell them that I should not come," Dr. Silla said tranquilly. "Therefore I did not let my change of plans trouble them. I suppose I was more tired than I knew – for after my final lecture, I thought why should I not take one of your English week-ends, before my long journey? Won't you sit down and eat your lunch with me? I see that you too have a basket, and you could not find a better place than this!"

Hilda sat down. Her mind was in a whirl, but her heart was at least no longer trying to get into her throat. She could still think, and she realized that if Dr. Silla had not gone to the Laboratory, her own visit there as an impostor would be undiscovered. She was – if not safe – at least in no immediate danger. Everything now depended upon whether Dr. Laing had discovered the loss of the tubes. If he had – Dr. Silla, as well as Hilda herself, was in danger. If he had *not*, both of them were still safe.

In any case it would be wiser to persuade Dr. Silla

to leave England immediately; there was an evening boat from Dover; but nobody Hilda had ever seen looked less easily persuadable than Dr. Silla.

"I have an idea," Dr. Silla said, finishing her sandwich, "that you English eat rather too much bread. Why on both sides of the ham, I ask myself always, with these ham-breads? Is it perhaps that the very strange yellow mustard is too strong—this Coleman's? Our ham-breads have either *no* mustard or just a *soupçon* of the less violent kind. I find that by the time I have accomplished the top piece of bread, as well as the lower one, I no longer taste the ham. Interesting this desire to hide a thing that tastes, by two pieces of something that do *not* taste? Is it perhaps a symbolical trait of the English mind?"

"How on earth," Hilda demanded, her attention unable to leave the core of their danger, "*did* you come here? I mean, where are you staying? Did you *know* I was here?"

"In a sense I did," Dr. Silla answered. "I had some more typing I wanted you to do for me on Monday. I was very well satisfied with your work, so I went to your office yesterday and your young clerk gave me your home address. I therefore went there, and your mother most kindly offered me a cup of tea, as well as giving me your present address. Had we not met in this unforeseen manner, I should have called upon you this afternoon. But this will do as well! Why do you not eat? Or is it that you have no lunch in that basket? My hotel has given me enough for two – take some of mine!"

Hilda gave a polite disclaimer and drew out her own lunch, and a bone for Archer. She could just be polite now, because, however strange it sounded, there was, she realized, no need for immediate action.

The outer world came comfortingly back to her, the keen sweet air, the vague scent of the little herbs they leaned against, the soft reassuring rustle of the small waves below them.

Hilda began to eat her lunch, quite as if Ronnie was not at the same moment probably eating his with Aunt Edith – three miles away.

Archer had taken to this calm, strange woman; after crunching his bone he ate what was left over of her substantial sandwiches, curled himself up in a ball at her feet, and slept.

Dr. Silla, having nothing to say, said nothing – absolutely nothing; nor did she even look as if she wanted to say anything. She wiped her fingers carefully with a paper napkin, and stared contentedly out to sea.

Hilda, on the other hand, found that she wanted to talk.

Here was an occasion when she might get a first-class psychological opinion upon her own problem, without having to get a ticket for it, or to listen to the less interesting problems of other people.

She had a friend, Hilda began by telling Dr. Silla, who was in a good deal of trouble, and had asked Hilda's advice. Hilda had thought a good deal about her friend's trouble, without being able to arrive at a satisfactory solution, and she would be very glad indeed if Dr. Silla could help her.

Dr. Silla was well accustomed to hear people with problems begin by stating that they were not their own; nor did she look as if she very much cared for exchanging the unprovocative simplicity of the sea for the complexities of a fellow human being. Still, she turned her wide-open candid eyes on Hilda's face, and answered her with friendliness.

"Since I do not know your friend, my opinion would be worth very little. You see people usually make a contribution to their own problems. Macbeth, for instance, would have had no problem had he had no ambition. The witches were no problem to Banquo, they were only a very curious spectacle. Therefore there are very few satisfactory answers to problems without a knowledge of the human beings who have caused them. Still, one often sees things more plainly by stating them to someone else – and I would be pleased to help you if I could. It is possible that after you have stated your friend's difficulty to me you may yourself see a way out of it. You have the advantage of me – since you know your friend."

"I know them all three," Hilda said hurriedly, "my friend – her sister – and – and her boy friend! At least he *was* hers! Now he isn't any more! He's the sister's! That's just the trouble!" Hilda pulled herself up short, and hesitated how to go on.

Dr. Silla removed her gaze, considerately, to the flight of a gull.

"The trouble wasn't exactly that either," Hilda went on after a pause; "the trouble was Ronnie!" Hilda paused again. She drew a deep breath, and looked away from Dr. Silla; away from Archer; away from the silver lightings of the gull's shifting wings, until her eyes settled upon the empty golden fields; but she did not see them; she saw instead, Ronnie; but that was no hallucination, for she knew that Ronnie was not there. She began to describe him. Ronnie was the trouble! An ordinary boy would not have mattered. Hilda's girl friend loved her sister – if her boy had been all right for *her*, he would have been all right for her sister. Hilda's girl friend would have been upset, of course – losing lovers *is* upsetting and losing one to a sister is more upsetting still – but not like that, not like what Hilda's friend felt now. She was not only upset – she was desperate! Because she knew what would happen to her sister. Her sister was delicate – she could not stand what Hilda's friend had already stood. Ronnie would first torture and then kill her. He would not mean to kill her, of course; but it would happen, since, whether he meant it or not, he always tortured the person that he loved. Well – that was her friend's problem! What should she do to stop her sister being tortured to death, before it was too late?

Dr. Silla's eyes met Hilda's. They demolished – and demolished in silence and with finality – Hilda's friend; there was simply Hilda.

"Perhaps," Dr. Silla said, when this complete unveiling had taken place between them, "perhaps now we'd both better be a little more real! Shall we not? Now to be tortured – that sometimes does happen between two human beings, and I can accept that it has happened to you – and might even happen to your sister, although not necessarily! I do not know your sister, but I could well imagine that she takes other people less seriously than you do! Has it not occurred to you that 'death' is an exaggerated effect for one person to have upon another? I have a feeling that this young man has greatly annoyed you, and could greatly annoy your sister – he is perhaps an ill-adjusted person. But I have not a feeling that he could cause the death of either of you! Also it is possible that, greatly as he has annoyed you, he might be less annoying to your sister.

"You see, Miss Fenchurch, you are a strong girl – you see clearly and with great emphasis – perhaps with an exaggerated emphasis – what goes on in yourself and others; and this boy friend – let us consider what you once found in him! Something to admire, was it not? And he perhaps needs admiration badly, and was very much lifted up because you gave him so much! Ill-adjusted men and women are like balloons. They rise on their vanity – and should it be suddenly punctured and the air let out, they naturally resent this process very much. Had you perhaps sometimes, without knowing it, punctured your boy friend's vanity? And your sister – would she be one of those who notice vanity in others, and who if they notice it, resent it? Even if she observed and resented it, would she not perhaps be one of those who do not puncture? I can assure you that a man can be most cruel to one woman, and quite favourable to another!

One must ask oneself always, how you both affected him?"

Hilda began to bite a piece of grass – it was old and dry, and not worth biting; still at the moment she preferred it to a better one. It was a new idea to her altogether, that Ronnie might be dangerous for her, and innocuous for Annie; nor was it at all a pleasurable idea. Still, Hilda had more honesty in her nature than she was herself aware of. She therefore entertained the unwelcome idea, without directly controverting it.

"Perhaps he might be nicer to Annie," she even admitted after a long pause; "but not in the end – because you see he would not want to marry a common girl, or, if he could help it, one without money. He has often told me so! That was the crab between Ronnie and me. For quite a long time he wanted us to be together. Anyhow he was always talking about a 'permanent arrangement'; as soon as he got his degree we meant to share a flat. Annie's prettier than me – and she's good. She won't *want* to let him be her lover, without marrying her – and if she lets him, she'll mind *more* – she'll mind horribly!"

"Ah!" said Dr. Silla, in a voice that somehow enormously comforted Hilda, "I have come across that before with English girls. Complete sexual purity is a very severe tradition – though I think that it goes better with early marriages, or with one of those serious love affairs that are a training for marriage. The economic question is the main difficulty. However, I understand this love affair of yours *was* serious?"

"It was very serious," Hilda agreed, "even with Ronnie it was serious, while it lasted! He said, and I think he meant, that he had never felt so safe with any woman before, except his mother; he said if he were dying, he would still want me – even afterwards; he – well, he sometimes said things like that!"

"Naturally," Dr. Silla said in a businesslike voice, entirely ignoring the sudden break in Hilda's. "Naturally, a strong woman is a protection. This boy had no doubt been over-mothered – perhaps cruelly over-mothered. He craves for a type from which he also rebels! He is now punishing you for this with Annie, and he must always punish you – for being stronger than he! Annie, he has not the same reason to punish, therefore he will never be *as* unkind to her as he has been to you. She will escape much! Even if he refuses to marry her – and remember this refusal may not stand; it depends upon what he desires most – if he really desires Annie, and she holds to her tradition of pre-marital purity, he may really marry her! And she *may* hold to it – for what strengthens such a tradition very materially is that it is also ungenerous. Weak natures have to be ungenerous! They are afraid of risks. This then will help your Annie to appear stronger than yourself. She may very well – just because she *is* weaker – refuse to be anything but a wife! There is a chastity produced by cowardice – just as there is a chastity produced by courage!"

"I've thought of that too," Hilda admitted in a low voice. "She might escape that. But think how she will suffer if she refuses him – and he deserts her! For Ronnie will desert her if he does not get what he wants! She has had T.B., and if she suffers, she is always ill. You see – she really *might* die! I wasn't *only* exaggerating."

"Possibly not," Dr. Silla said tolerantly. "One is usually exaggerating for some other reason, but one avoids the truth by it, all the same! However, since you have given a great deal more thought to this problem than I have, and also have the advantage of knowing well all those whom it concerns – what solution has hitherto occurred to you – to try?"

Hilda produced Aunt Edith. "He's with her now," she explained. "Aunt Edith is in some ways rather wonderful. For one thing she could talk a dog's hind leg off. But I don't mean only that. I mean Ronnie'll *have* to see she's a real personality, and be impressed by her mind. She's clever in the same way *he* is! So I had a feeling that it might *just* come off. On the other hand of course it might not! That's why I asked you."

"Well," Dr. Silla said, carefully wrapping up her scraps, and replacing them in the basket, "I could tell you better *after* we know what your Aunt Edith has succeeded in accomplishing. It may be that we need do nothing more. In any case, however, I should be pleased if you would come to breakfast with me, in my hotel, to-morrow at nine o'clock. It is called 'Kingsway,' and is only a mile from here. Meantime will you agree *not* to act, until we have talked further? Whether your Aunt Edith fails or succeeds? If the problem has been solved, we shall eat our bacon and eggs and drink our good English tea in peace, as well as in comfort! If she has failed, then we think together again! But of one thing I feel perfectly sure — that neither you nor your sister will die because of this young man's fancies. His is the failure — not yours! And you are to be congratulated that he *has* failed finally to impress you!"

Hilda gazed at her in astonishment. "But — but," she stammered, "surely it is I who failed — failed, I mean, to impress — or to hold Ronnie?"

Dr. Silla took up her basket and brushed the crumbs from her black dress — it was the same one that she had lectured in. She had others, but not any so smart, and she had wished to be smart when she arrived in Paris to meet Cornelius. Since she had given up this plan, she had not yet had time to unpack her other clothes. Fortunately the crumbs were dry, and had done the black dress no great harm.

"To fail in being loved by a light young man is surely a fortunate occurrence," Dr. Silla said, holding out her hand to Hilda, with her friendly, childlike smile. "I congratulate you highly upon it! There are many nice serious young men who would be ashamed to offer a woman false coinage! No doubt, in time, you will attract and be attracted by one of them. *Auf Wiedersehen.*" And with a final pat to Archer, Dr. Silla left Hilda, standing quite still, at the edge of the cliff, looking after her.

Chapter 14

WHEN Hilda reached the bungalow, she found it empty. The key was in its usual place under the mat, accompanied by a letter from her Aunt Edith.

Please see that Archer has plenty to drink after his long walk. I have to help the Vicar with the Girl Guides – his wife has a bilious attack as usual. She doesn't understand girls, and crocks up on purpose, I believe, on *my* Saturdays – but it can't be helped. I'll be back as soon after tea as I can. Everything else when we meet! Love – EDITH.

"Everything else when we meet," sounded a little vague to Hilda; it almost sounded as if Aunt Edith, who was as a rule quite definite, had *wished* to be a little vague.

The bungalow had been left in perfect order: the lunch things washed up, and put away, the cushions shaken; but the smoke of Ronnie's favourite cigarettes still lingered in the air.

Hilda gave Archer his drink and refused to play ball with him rather curtly; then she went back into the sitting-room where the smoke still lingered.

It was the kind of room Ronnie would like, pleasantly austere. The furniture was plain unpolished wood; the colours were pale and clear, the bookshelves well stocked; there was a good print or two on the walls; a black divan deep in cushions; a wood-ply floor; only a rug in front of the roomy fireplace. No inglenook, or pouffes. Ten years ago Aunt Edith had had both these iniquities; but she had shaken them off with the years. The room was now enlightened eighteenth century. She even had a sampler on the wall called "The Children's Friend," in woolwork: A chestnut-coloured dog of convenient size, but indefinite as to race, was pulling a child out of a stream by a garment of bright pink wool that, though presumably wet through, stood up on purpose like wire netting. An enchanting white-feather tree bloomed under a glass case in the centre of the room. Photographs were banned; and all vases, except a black wooden bowl, with one rose floating gingerly on the surface.

There was only one easy chair in the room; and Hilda knew that in the end Ronnie would have sat in it. She seemed to see him drooping gracefully against the cushions; his crossed leg wagging freely, his long thin hands moving rapidly as he talked. Ronnie always poured himself into chairs, as if he were made of milk.

He was the sort of talker who begins very diffidently, with little shy rushes of speech; and Aunt Edith would be sure to feel that she must soothe, and draw him out; but she would not draw anything out that Ronnie had not already *meant* her to draw out.

Hilda sighed a little wearily; it was to be hoped that Aunt Edith would stick to the facts, but what she might not quite grasp was what Ronnie habitually did with facts – he "broke them up," as they say at Hollywood with their chosen subjects, "to make a picture"; and by the time he had regrouped the pieces, they bore very little likeness to the original theme.

Hilda seemed to see Ronnie, for the first time today, shorn of his ancient glamour. She felt oddly free; and strangely lonely in her sense of freedom.

She did not know what she was going to do with

herself, but she felt that she had more of a self to do things with. All through her long and bitter loving, she had made herself into a channel for expressing Ronnie's wishes. Now she suddenly felt that she might one day discover that she had wishes of her own to express.

What had happened, Hilda asked herself wonderingly, to that nostalgic ache that used to take possession of her body and soul, whenever she was confronted by the bare traces of Ronnie's vanished presence?

This was the cushion his head had pressed; this was the chair from which he had surveyed Aunt Edith and her background; he would have stood by the bookcase, and fingered its contents, while his quick eyes ran over their titles. He would have strolled to the window, and looked between the rigid, plain yellow curtains towards the faint line of the sea.

She could still see him doing these things, but something had happened to Ronnie's figure. Although it was still in the centre of Hilda's mind it was less intimate, and less impressive.

Hilda had intended to stay in the sitting-room, and have no tea; but she felt now as if she would like to go into the kitchen and make some for herself. After drinking her tea, Hilda actually agreed to play ball with Archer; and was still playing with him when she heard the leisurely chunk of Aunt Edith's baby Austin approaching "Honeymead."

Aunt Edith drew up at the exact gate of the middle bungalow, and jumped out.

She was immediately swallowed up in the torrential welcome of Archer. Hilda wondered if she was mistaken in thinking that Aunt Edith needlessly prolonged Archer's rhapsodies?

Hilda thought that Aunt Edith wore an uneasily cheerful expression, like that of a person who wants to persuade you, in advance, that the somewhat doubtful news she brings is wholly good.

Eventually they sat down together on two steamer chairs, outside the French windows. There was a pink-and-golden glow over the western sky. Aunt Edith drew attention to it; took out her cigarette-case, offered one to Hilda, who refused it, and lit her own; then she became needlessly witty about Girl Guides.

At last Hilda broke out with impatience: "Well, Aunt Edith, I suppose Ronnie *did* turn up after all?"

"Oh, yes, of course!" Aunt Edith said with exaggerated eagerness. "I am going to tell you everything about his visit, Hilda dear, directly! I know *just* how you feel! Only I always think one must be in the right mood for a *real* talk. This business of you and Ronnie is all so complicated – and in a sense awkward! One always thinks a love affair is going to last for ever, but thank God it doesn't. You remember that French proverb: *'Tout casse; tout lasse; tout passe! Telle est la vie!'* "

"Yes," said Hilda dryly, "I remember it. Did you get Ronnie to say he'd leave Annie alone?"

"How you jump at things, darling!" Aunt Edith said a little reproachfully. "Ronnie and I are both sophisticated, experienced people, and naturally we discussed the whole affair in that spirit. There was no crude *i*-dotting between us. And yet, I think I may say that, before he left, Ronnie had fully understood what the possibilities of the situation are – and er – are *not!* Certainly you need not be in the least afraid for little Annie – that will work itself out, I am sure, *quite* all right!"

Hilda sat up with a jerk, always a difficult and ungraceful thing to do in a steamer chair, and remained sitting bolt upright. Her eyes fixed themselves, with the pertinacity of gimlets, upon Aunt Edith's flushed face. Aunt Edith looked a trifle less cheerful; and called unnecessarily to Archer to keep off the grass, since for a long time Archer had seen to it that there was no grass to keep off.

Hilda saw quite plainly what had happened. Ronnie had diddled Aunt Edith. She might have known he would! After an hour of Ronnie, against a lifetime of Hilda, Aunt Edith could say, and not see how she gave herself away by saying it: "Ronnie and I"! Like Balaam, without the excuse of the ass, Aunt Edith had set out to curse, and found her mouth strangely full of blessings!

"I see what happened," Hilda exclaimed with brutal directness. "Ronnie fooled you! Well, I didn't think it of you, Aunt Edith. I thought you'd hold on to what Ronnie really *did* – not to the stuff he'd ladle out to you – to hide it! He's messed up my life, and he's going to mess up Annie's! Wasn't that enough for you? What's the use of your saying you always stand by women, when the first boy you meet has only got to flatter you, for you to cave right in?

"The truth is you cared more about making a good impression on Ronnie than you did about saving Annie! Well, I know where we are now, at any rate!"

"Hilda!" exclaimed Aunt Edith, with the blustering fury of one whose conscience cannot wholly support its indignation, "how *dare* you speak to me like that! All that I did was done for you and Annie! This young man is a perfect stranger to me – think of that expensive fish, and cream with the peaches! And I invited him to lunch, *although* it was Polly's *one* whole day out a month – and you know I never think of changing it! To say nothing of giving up my Saturday to you and your friend – working hard as I do, with all my own personal friends longing to see me! How can you suppose I *want* to spend my time helping you out of a most disagreeable love affair you ought never to have got into?"

"How have you helped me out?" Hilda demanded implacably. "You felt so badly about the same roof, when I told you last night – have you got Ronnie to change it? If he'd go away without Mums knowing why, it would be something!"

Aunt Edith sought for control, and found some of it. "In a sense," she said stiffly, "it's extraordinarily good of Ronnie to remain! He'd far *rather* leave; he said so, when I pointed out the desirability of his being – elsewhere. He's thinking of your father and mother, and their financial difficulties! Naturally – under the circumstances – he'd *prefer* to leave the house!"

"Why?" Hilda asked rudely. "Under what other circumstances would he get for thirty shillings a week, which Mums lets him run on for months without paying, the kind of food and care and special treatment he has with us? The best room in the house too, and his errands done for him? I think *not*, Aunt Edith – I think Ronnie'd prefer to *stay!* And I know well enough that if he *didn't* prefer it, he'd be out of the house to-morrow!"

"It's you that he wishes to avoid!" Aunt Edith said, with two spots of burning red on her cheek-bones, and the hand that held her cigarette trembling violently. "It's *your* behaviour, Hilda, that has forced him into a position no gentleman can comfortably stand! Ronnie – poor boy – found that he could tell *me* what he suffers – man to man, as it were! It's very painful for me to have to repeat this to you, but you oblige me to speak plainly. Ronnie said that you had made the situation quite impossible for him – by your – well, by your passionate behaviour! He blamed himself for not having resisted you, to start with – but after all, he's a man – with a man's temptations!"

"Oh, no, he isn't," Hilda interrupted viciously. "He's the innocent victim of a nymphomaniac! Look here, Aunt Edith, you've known me ever since I was born – you've seen me with men, and you've seen me without them; have I ever shown any such symptoms? You're a woman who knows girls – what makes you think (for you always *have* thought I was decently normal about men and have often said so!) that Ronnie knows me better than you do?"

Aunt Edith, brought up short like this, face to face with her own past wisdom, felt extremely uncomfortable.

She had, as a matter of fact, expressed a similar doubt – though better worded – to Ronnie. She remembered exactly what she had said, but she felt disinclined to repeat it to Hilda. Her own words had been: "But I've never seen the least sign of anything oversexed in Hilda! If either of them *were*, I should have said it was Annie. *She* has always shown a decided preference for men's society – and has lots of them hanging round her, in a provocative way. But Hilda – never!" Ronnie had replied with an almost *reverent* look, as if Aunt Edith were the only *wholly* immaculate woman he had ever met: "But, my dear Miss Fenchurch, you'd be the very *last* person in the world before whom Hilda *would* show such tendencies!"

This role of unsullied purity Aunt Edith not only had every right to play, but enjoyed playing; still, it is difficult to combine it simultaneously with that other role of experienced, unshockable woman of the world; and while talking to Hilda Aunt Edith had a moment of frenzied indecision, between the two parts, before she closed with the latter.

"I don't suppose you realize, Hilda," she said gravely, "how difficult a young girl – and you were an *innocent* young girl then – *can* make things for a man, who is actually staying in the same *house* with her!"

"Oh yes, I do," Hilda replied with bitter irony. "You forget my pronounced passions! After successfully attacking Ronnie's virtue, they wouldn't, you know, become any *less* pronounced! I have had to control – and *still* have to control them – while living in the same house! There's nothing you and Ronnie can tell me about controlling passions, that *I* don't know; and from a personal experience which I understand *you've* managed to avoid! As for Ronnie, he's never controlled the slightest wish, even for a sugar cake – and is not likely to begin now! No! We'd better leave all that primeval stuff alone, Aunt Edith. It doesn't cut any ice in this affair anyhow! If Mums and Dad *knew* what I told you last night, they'd hoof Ronnie out of the house to-morrow; but they don't know it, and it wouldn't do any good, as far as Annie's future is concerned, to tell them. They'd only make an awful row, and after it was over she'd go on seeing Ronnie just the same, only without telling them! My own case is over and done with. What smoke there is left, I'll consume — so don't you worry! I only told you about it, to show you that it might be more serious still for Annie, and to get you to help her out of it. I thought you might be able to make Ronnie see that he'd better leave us — on his own — *without* being turned out, and I thought he might feel he couldn't treat Annie as he's treated me, once he saw he'd got you to deal with. Ronnie turned your head, Aunt Edith, and you may be sure he *saw* that he'd turned it! You can't do any good now. I trusted you to take our parts, but you had to cut a figure with Ronnie instead. Well, cutting figures and helping other people don't go together! And I can't trust you any more — that's all there is to it!"

Aunt Edith felt as if the words she had assembled in her mind — wise, kind, soothing words — had been wiped off her lips by some unknown power. Still, perhaps she could have reassembled them, had not Hilda leaned forward, with her head on her arms, and begun to sob in the most awful way, not proper crying, but hard, dry, tearless sobs that shook her whole body. She made hardly any sound, but she swayed and sobbed, sobbed and swayed, as if she were possessed by a devil. It was still clear daylight, and "Honeymead" stood between two other bungalows — "Polders End" on one side of it, and "Syren's Song" on the other. Fortunately everybody was having tea inside, because of the wind; still they might, any of them, come out, at any moment.

"You'd better go indoors, Hilda," Aunt Edith urged anxiously, "if you've *got* to go on like that – we're so overlooked here!" Hilda seemed to have to go on like that; but she came to herself sufficiently to go on like it inside. Staggering into the living-room she flung herself face downwards on the black divan, clutching at the cushions, as if she were trying to strangle them.

Aunt Edith forgot Hilda's cruel and utterly unjustifiable words; for the moment all she could remember was that Hilda was her favourite niece, in a trouble that she herself – when you came right down to it – had done nothing to mend.

Those elated, smooth-sailing, skilful hours with Ronnie, faded into complete insignificance. Aunt Edith gazed unhappily, and for once uncertainly, at the back of Hilda's head. She even pushed Archer out into the garden, and shut the French window on him, because he went up to the divan and sniffed suspiciously at Hilda's unexpected posture.

Aunt Edith was still certain, *morally* certain – she told herself – that Ronnie had far too much respect for her to seduce Annie. Besides he had told her that, with Annie, there was simply no such question. There *had* been such a question with Hilda; but Hilda had provided both the question and the answer. Besides when the accident happened, Ronnie had not yet seen Aunt Edith. Still how could Aunt Edith explain this to Hilda in a convincing or soothing way when Hilda had gone so far beyond the use of reason? Her feet were drumming the black divan, in such a tempestuous and abandoned manner, that Aunt Edith felt quite worried about the springs; but she felt more worried still about Hilda.

She sat down close to the divan, and lit another cigarette. Aunt Edith was beginning to blame herself, for not having been colder and firmer; and less interested in Ronnie.

"Will you listen to me for a moment, Hilda?" she said quietly; and to her relief and surprise, Hilda stopped sobbing, and listened.

"I mayn't have done *all* I meant to do this afternoon," Aunt Edith admitted in a strangely shaken voice; "perhaps I *did* pay too much attention to Ronnie's charming manners! I'm very sorry if I've failed you; but *honestly*, *honestly*, Hilda I have a feeling that Ronnie won't! I meant won't do anything like – like that – with Annie! I – I think I *did* make that quite plain to him. Really and truly, I *tried* to do that for you!"

Hilda sat up; her face was less distorted. She pushed back her heavy red hair with both her hands, and even tried to smile.

"Sorry, Aunt Edith," she muttered. "I didn't mean to lose my head like that! Only he's done it so often, and he always gets away with it! I'm afraid it isn't any use having feelings about what Ronnie'll do – or *not* do. If he wants Annie more than he minds being bothered by it, he'll *take* her; and if not – not! Nothing you or I can say, or anyone else for that matter, is going to be any help at all! I ought to have known that, and not have asked you to take on the job!

"Now I'll go upstairs, and tidy up, and then help you get supper. But it's no use talking about Ronnie any more!"

Aunt Edith could not feel that Hilda was right. She was unable to imagine a situation when talking was not the best possible thing to do; but she was so relieved that Hilda had stopped that awful sobbing that she was quite glad to let her have her own way, for the moment; besides Aunt Edith felt and went on feeling quite extraordinarily uncomfortable; almost as if she *had*, and *knew* that she had, preferred her personal vanity to her niece's need. Hilda had not meant *only* to be cruel, when she had said: "Well, I can't trust you any more – that's all there is to it!" She had spoken as one speaks when one has been defrauded. Aunt Edith had been a force in Hilda's life – perhaps not quite so strong or so beneficent a force as she had pictured herself as being, but still a force; and now she was a force no more! There was something else as bad as this, that followed from it, and Aunt Edith's mind – which was an extremely good one – reached this point directly after Hilda had left the room. What would the poor child do, besides washing her hands and face, and coming down to supper? What do people do who have props removed from them, in moments of adversity?

They have to do without them, Aunt Edith a little grimly reminded herself.

Nor would she have found any more satisfactory answer to this question had her eyes been able to see through the flimsy doors, and an unsubstantial flooring, to where Hilda was standing with her bag open in her hand, staring hard at two small, neatly packed tubes. "I shall have to use them *now*, all right," Hilda told herself, closing the bag with a decisive snap, "directly I get home." It was the first time Hilda had seen herself using them.

Chapter 15

AFTER making up her mind to kill Ronnie, Hilda slept straight through the night for the first time for weeks. The driving force of her will had fought her exhausted heart to a standstill.

Aunt Edith too, when Hilda came downstairs, was like wax in her hands. She did not allow herself a single protest when she heard that Hilda, instead of accompanying her to an early service, had made an engagement to take breakfast at a strange hotel with a foreign lady who was both a psychological lecturer and a Czechoslovakian – exactly the kind of person Aunt Edith told herself that she was most capable of coping with, one who would be thrown away upon a mere chit like Hilda. Aunt Edith was an Anglo-

Catholic and, though remarkably broad-minded, as many of these persons are (being on the whole more Anglo than Catholic), she naturally liked her favourite niece to go to early services with her, returning full of sea air and spirituality, to a special Sunday breakfast of bacon and tomatoes.

This morning, however, she listened to Hilda's explosive plan with calculated meekness, merely saying gently, after rather a long pause: "Archer gets so wild on Sundays at not being able to go with me to church – I suppose you couldn't very well take him with you?"

Touched by having so much latitude shown her, Hilda accepted Archer's company.

It was even something of a relief, to have him larking rhetorically round her, at evasive gulls. Heavy dew lay on the empty fields, silvering the edges of scarlet brambles and slipping its jewelled radiance into cobwebs. The sea and sky were a milky lightless blue. Sounds carried far in the still air; larks were already singing; mechanically, Hilda thought, with the wearying reiteration of electric bells.

Hilda had a curious, hunted feeling, that was not exactly fright, and yet which made her feel, when she saw a coastguard walking casually along the cliff's edge, as if she had no right upon the public path.

She turned over in her mind the best way of persuading Dr. Silla not to go up to town again before leaving England. Perhaps Dr. Silla, who liked sea air, and appeared to like Hilda, would agree to letting Hilda do her work here? Once Dr. Silla went to London anything might happen. Even though it looked as if the disappearance of the tubes had been safely overlooked, since the papers said nothing about them and such losses are usually widely advertised, there was still the risk of somebody solving Dr. Silla's rightful identity, and starting up the question that if this were Dr. Silla who had Hilda been?

Yesterday, Hilda had felt startled and shocked by Dr. Silla's sudden appearance, but the questions themselves had not had this grim intensity. Yesterday Hilda had still thought she was not going to need the contents of the tubes. Yesterday, the facts were the same, but the criminal intent had not hardened into certainty.

Archer's lithe body, darting here and there after his effortlessly escaping prey, was filled with the resilient ecstasy of the summer morning; but Hilda felt none of Archer's carefree innocence. "Shall I go on feeling half dead and alone – all my life?" she asked herself desperately. "Ronnie does no one anything but harm – it's like putting an end to a poisonous snake to kill him! How else can he *be* got rid of – if he won't go away?" But there is a lie in all analogies and Hilda knew that Ronnie was a man and not a snake. Once again she felt the hot, trembling rage take possession of her, the rage she had felt the night before when she heard what Ronnie had said of her to Aunt Edith.

Those hard sobs that had frightened Aunt Edith had not been sorrow. They had been the physical reaction of a burning, blinding rage; a rage that knew itself impotent.

All women value their virginity, but Hilda had set upon hers a special value – partly because she was a self-respecting, physically fastidious girl, and partly because Mums had always made such a terrific point of personal purity. "It's different for men," Mums had told her, when the question first came up. "They're respectable enough if they're honest about money – that's what they think the most of – and you can't blame them, as it's what their wives and families have got to live on; but a girl's virtue is her only real property; and though it's all right being married – and no more than natural, as you'll find when the time comes – giving way to a man till you're married is *never* right! You get nothing whatever for it, and you lose all you've got – no matter what they tell you!"

Even when Hilda found that younger, and presumably wiser, people than Mums took the question of chastity with an agreeable lightness, something fixed and firm within herself never responded to their lightness.

When Hilda had first loved Ronnie, she had not envisaged any such surrender. It had been the price that in the end, after her whole being had become involved in Ronnie's pleasure, she had had to pay in order to keep him.

Ronnie had been quite clear about it. "A love affair," he told her, "has to be thorough! You do – or you don't! As for marriage, it's just a terrific plant that girls drag men into, so as to get paid for all their lives! And for a thing, mind you, that they ought never to *be* paid for at all! I'm sure *you're* not the mercenary type, but if you are – I clear out on the spot!"

This sounded so convincing and, at the same time, the role it gave Hilda to play was so high-minded that she could not hold out against it. From that moment she had refused Ronnie nothing.

To realize that he himself did not believe in

the high ideal of disinterested love that he had set before her, but could think of her, and paint her for others, as an uncontrolled and vicious wanton, roused in Hilda a rage so deep that she felt neither regret nor remorse for anything she was going to do to him.

This odd feeling that made the summer air taste unclean had surely nothing to do with Ronnie?

"I don't mind *what* he suffers," Hilda told herself fiercely, "he deserves it! I'm only afraid now, I suppose, because I don't want to be hanged *for* killing him! Well – then I must just take care not to *be* hanged, that's all!" But her deepening sense of loneliness denied that it was all. It was a relief to be confronted suddenly with the pleasant imitation Tudor hotel where Dr. Silla was staying.

A bed of geraniums bloomed in front of it and, the sun having been on them for nearly an hour, the air was filled by their delicious, pungent scent.

Dr. Silla had actually induced a deeply disapproving waiter to lay a table for them outside the dining-room window, close to the geraniums; and she was already sitting at it, reading a Sunday paper, when Archer forced himself upon her recognition.

She greeted Hilda cordially; and said that she did not mind Archer. The waiter, who *did* mind Archer but could not very well say so, brought out a list of breakfast dishes that contained bacon and tomatoes with small sausages thrown in; and Hilda sat down, and began to eat, without feeling hungry. She did feel, however, vaguely pleased to see Dr. Silla.

Dr. Silla had very little to say for herself, until they had finished their breakfast; then she suggested that they should take chairs and sit in a quiet corner of the garden.

People were beginning to come out of the hotel, in a pleasant, objectless, Sunday morning manner.

Some of the younger ones strolled off to the tennis-courts, on the other side of a hedge that surrounded the pocket handkerchief of lawn, upon which they sat.

Older men strolled out with even less determination, but after brief exchanges of suggestion, melted comfortably and easily away in small cars, with bags of golf clubs beside them.

A few middle-aged women, with still controllable children, set out in their Sunday best, across the fields to church. Bells pealed across the sunny cornfields, with a happy chime.

"Do you believe in God?" Hilda demanded rather jerkily.

Dr. Silla was smoking serenely, and patting anything of Archer that happened to come her way. She turned her head a little, to meet Hilda's remark.

"What kind of god do you mean?" she asked cautiously. "In Czechoslovakia we often paint a large eye on the trunk of a tree, or you will find a thickly bearded old gentleman leaning out over the front doors of farmhouses, supported to the waist by clouds, and pointing a warning finger at you – in such a god, I do *not* believe!"

"I suppose I did mean that kind," Hilda murmured uneasily; "because if you mean the other – a sort of Push that started everything up, you can't very well do much about it, can you?"

"No," Dr. Silla agreed, after a silent puff or two, "I don't suppose you can." After another rather long silence, she added, "*Must* you?"

"Well," Hilda answered, more uneasily still, "I've always supposed you *must!* If there is a God – then you've *got* to be good! I suppose that's the general idea. And if not – and mind you, I've never seriously thought there was – then it's up to you, and *isn't* so important!"

"I should have supposed that if it is up to you, it would be *more* important," Dr. Silla said slowly. "That one should do anything about God, if He exists, I have never supposed necessary; but that one should *do* something about man – I have taken for granted. I think there is often quite a lot to do about man – and some of it not always very agreeable! Still he is our brother!"

After a moment's silence, Dr. Silla went on, as if it were part of the same subject: "There is your personal problem, for instance! I should like very much to hear what you are doing about that? And if you found your Aunt Edith could be of use to you and your sister?"

Hilda hesitated. She had really started the idea of God because He seemed a safely abstract subject, brought up by the sound of the church-bells. She had no idea He could so easily become a part of her personal activities. Besides, since she had made up her mind what to do, her problem – in the light of a problem – had ceased to exist. She had forgiven her Aunt Edith; but there was not very much to say about Aunt Edith's interview with Ronnie which would not sound like giving Aunt Edith away. "It didn't pan out very well," she at last admitted. "You see, Ronnie fools people – even very clever people like my Aunt Edith – he knows how – and they don't think he does. He just seems a nice, helpless boy to them – helpless about life, I mean – but awfully amusing and witty. Aunt Edith meant to help me, but she got side-tracked."

"I see," Dr. Silla dispassionately observed. "I did not tell you, I think, yesterday, but while I was calling on your mother, to ask for your address, Ronnie came in. Your father and your sister Annie, I did not see; but I have had some conversation with your friend – Ronnie."

"Oh," Hilda exclaimed, feeling as if she were being shot up too fast in a lift, "did you? No! Of course, I didn't know you'd ever seen – Ronnie!" It somehow or other made an overwhelming difference to Hilda that Dr. Silla had seen Ronnie. It made her seem much nearer.

"Yes," Dr. Silla went on meditatively, "and I received a very poor impression of him – very poor indeed! I am surprised that you should think at all seriously of Ronnie! Such a young man should carry no weight at all with a well-balanced person."

"Perhaps I am not a well-balanced person," Hilda said stiffly, for she felt curiously offended at this low estimate of Ronnie. She might wish to kill him, but she did not wish to be told that he was not impressive.

Dr. Silla made no reply. She sat blinking in the sun, as if it did not really matter to her whether Hilda was a well-balanced person or not.

After a long but upon her part obviously comfortable pause, Dr. Silla murmured: "But I see that you have already arrived at a decision – so there is no further need for us to discuss your problem."

"How did you guess I had?" Hilda demanded incredulously. "I haven't said so!"

"Yesterday," Dr. Silla reminded Hilda, "you were anxious for my opinion. To-day you no longer seek it. It seems reasonable to suppose that in the interval you have solved your problem to your own satisfaction."

Hilda sat silent for a long time. Yesterday she had suffered severely from Aunt Edith's inability to discern or even, when she had discerned, to speak the truth; now she found herself suffering more severely still from a person who discerned the truth very easily indeed, and spoke nothing else.

"Well," Hilda admitted at last, "in a sense I have decided what to do. I don't know that it's particularly satisfactory – but I *have* decided."

Dr. Silla asked no further questions, and Hilda began to feel a little cheap and flat. For one thing she had eaten an expensive breakfast, and taken up Dr. Silla's time, on false pretences.

Dr. Silla had begun to hum, and there is something about humming that suggests that a conversation has come to an end. Perhaps, Hilda thought, she ought to go, and yet, strangely enough, she felt very disinclined to leave the sunny garden. Talking about oneself, too, is so absorbing an occupation, when one is not interrupted by another person's talking about herself, that Hilda found it hard to put an end to it before it had fairly begun. She could not go yet, Hilda reminded herself, not until she had prevented Dr. Silla's return to London.

"It seems a pity," she began cautiously, "as I suppose you're sailing from Dover, for you to have to go back to London at all? I can easily stay on here another day or two, and do any typewriting you want, on the spot. Aunt Edith has a machine, and her holiday is over, so that, as she's out all day at her training college, we could use the bungalow. Mums wanted me to stay longer, anyhow, and if I've got work to do here, it won't matter missing what might turn up in London."

"I have about four hours' work I can give you," Dr. Silla promptly replied, without dragging in the question of whether she meant it to be in London, or near Dover.

The silence closed round them again, more formidably than ever. The bells had stopped chiming. Dr. Silla ceased to hum. The breakfast things were cleared away. No more motors came or went, over the neatly combed gravel drive.

Only from the tennis-court came the shrill intermittent cries of the players. The word "Love" broke with a sickening reiteration upon Hilda's mind.

It made her say at last, desperately and without volition: "There's only one thing to do now – as far as I can see – and that's to kill Ronnie!"

"You might kill yourself," Dr. Silla suggested, with her eyes fixed upon Archer, who was carrying on a determined flea-hunt in a disadvantageous position.

"I might of course," Hilda answered, "but I'm a bread-winner, and there's Mums. I couldn't possibly upset her like that!"

"It might upset her a good deal more if you were hanged," Dr. Silla remarked casually. "The police, over here, are, I believe, very efficient; and murder is a crime that people are always anxious to see solved."

"Yes, but supposing that I knew *how* to do it," Hilda went on defensively, for she felt her pride at stake, "*without* being found out?"

"You'd have to be very clever indeed," Dr. Silla replied rather dryly, "*not* to get found out."

Again Hilda felt creep over her that cold and lonely feeling she had waked up with, as if she were cut off from the young men in flannels, and the young girls in their short white skirts, flashing to and fro, through the gaps in the hedge. ("I can never do *that* any more," she told herself.)

"Even if you weren't found out," the inexorable, unemphatic voice beside her went on, "I can imagine that you might feel more uncomfortable than it is necessary for anyone to feel. You would have taken away another person's right to live."

"Has Ronnie any right to live – like that?" Hilda demanded fiercely.

"No – not like that," Dr. Silla agreed; "but even his having no 'right' is his own business. He might at any time see his mistake, and alter his way of living. We are at the mercy of our opinion of ourselves, but that opinion can be changed – by ourselves – or sometimes by events – or sometimes by others! Criminals are less final than their punishments. After people are dead, of course, one can sum up the whole of what they have left, and if they have left nothing, then nothing is exactly what they were worth. But before they are dead, one is in no position to judge; and I should not myself care to push another person into that abyss of nothingness!"

"But is nothingness worse than the kind of things Ronnie does?" Hilda pleaded. "He says awful things about his mother and father, who adore him! I used to think them true – until I found out that he said the same kind of things against other people that I *knew* weren't true. He made fun of Mums till I stopped him, and he does things that are so mean! He borrows and doesn't pay back, even when he knows how poor people are, and he – well, I don't know – he seems to turn everything the wrong way, whenever he wants to – and then get out of having done it!"

"But have you ever asked yourself," Dr. Silla demanded, "how bad you were for Ronnie? You see, there is in all human relationships a switch-back element – one up, one down, unless the weight is even! Do you not think that you may have switched Ronnie down, far below his natural level – and so be responsible, yourself, for some of his errors? He is a lighter weight than you, and, while you were so fascinated by him, you must have swung him very high, and forced him correspondingly low, when you withheld your adoration?"

"What a very curious way of looking at things!" Hilda said, in a low uncertain voice. It had certainly never occurred to her, when, goaded by Ronnie's weaknesses, she had let fall her drastic criticisms, that she was undermining what little strength Ronnie had. She said a little defensively: "What I told him was true, Dr. Silla! I mean, he'd always done and said the things I brought home to him!"

"To be in the right is often an expensive business," Dr. Silla murmured, "and does one always know what *is* true? In the same way I am very often told by indiscreet people, 'I always say what I think!' But do such people know how to think?"

Hilda sat for a while in silence, rather a stubborn silence. She resented the idea that she could have done harm to Ronnie. All her wrongs surged through her again; and she encouraged their surging.

Dr. Silla's attention concentrated itself upon Archer, who, growing restive, was bringing her stones to throw for him.

Dr. Silla refused to throw stones. She explained to Archer that stones would hurt his teeth; and told him that he would only get sticks thrown. She put in front of herself a stone and a stick, and each time Archer presented her with the stone, she took up the stick and threw it; and when he refused to return it, and brought her another stone, Dr. Silla replaced the stone by a fresh stick from the hedge behind her, and threw that; until at last the idea dawned upon Archer that he would only get sticks thrown, and he gave up bringing her back stones.

Hilda grew more and more irritated by what seemed to her an unkind and useless absorption on the part of a friend. Dr. Silla should have been anxious to convince Hilda, not to convince Archer, who would quite probably by to-morrow have forgotten the lesson, and return to stones.

At last Hilda burst out with a statement she had not intended to reveal.

"I never posted your letter!" she said defiantly. Dr. Silla told Archer, with a finality that he actually accepted, that he had had enough even of sticks. She looked straight at Hilda. "I know that you did not post my letter," she said quietly. "That is the reason why I did not go to Paris as soon as I had intended."

"What!" Hilda exclaimed, springing to her feet. "You knew – and you never asked me why? Then – what?" but without finishing her question, she sank back into her chair again. She felt bewildered, and aghast; but suddenly no longer alone.

"You see," Dr. Silla explained painstakingly, once Hilda had settled down again, "you gave me the impression that you were reliable; and I saw by your face, when I recognized you in the lecture hall, that you felt ashamed. Since there was no other question at stake between us except that of posting or not posting my letter, of what else could you feel ashamed than of not posting it? It was very easy to guess that you had *not* posted it! But *why* you had not posted it, that was of course not so easy. I decided to wait and see. When unreliable people do not do what they have promised, it is very easy to understand that they should fail—to be unreliable is, as the French say, their *métier!* But if a reliable person does not do what she has undertaken, there must be some important reason for it. It even seemed to me that this reason might be of sufficient importance for me to postpone my journey. You see, it concerned me, since it would seem, if you had *not* posted the letter, a great failure of courtesy on my part to my colleagues, neither to accept nor to explain why I could *not* accept their invitation to visit the Laboratory!"

"I see," Hilda said after a long pause. "Yes – I see! I had no right to make you fail them!" Dr. Silla did not contradict Hilda's statement; she seemed to accept it, rather as a fact than as a self-accusation.

"I was so upset," Hilda went on, after a pause. "I didn't mean to put you in the wrong, Dr. Silla, I just – well – what I'd planned to do was so terrible that the part about posting the letter didn't seem of any importance!"

"To you it was not important," Dr. Silla agreed tranquilly, "but to me it was important."

Hilda sat crouched forward in her chair, staring hard at the rail of green hedge between them and the tennis players.

She felt an overpowering desire to tell this strange woman everything. Dr. Silla's judgments were devastatingly clear – they left no loop-hole of escape, but they were without hostility – they seemed to belong to a region that had no stigma of superiority. If Hilda said, "I am a murderer – I mean to kill Ronnie!" Dr. Silla would neither disembarrass her of the guilt of murder, nor side with the pack of the world in regarding Hilda as an enemy. There was, however, a real danger in telling Dr. Silla, the danger that having told her, Hilda might not be able to go on with the murder. Something curious said or thought by Dr. Silla might stop her; and Hilda's mind was made up – her will was already in operation. She was running steadily, between blinkers, towards her goal.

After a long pause, Hilda said, "If I saw any other way – but I don't!"

"Any other way than to kill Ronnie?" Dr. Silla asked with sobriety but without reproach. "As a doctor, I cannot of course agree with you. My business has always seemed to me to fight death and to prolong life – even, I sometimes admit, in the case of grievous and inexorable pain, a little unreasonably! Is it not the business of all strong persons – since death is certainly a retreat into nothingness – to increase a dying person's incentive to live? To let a person die has always seemed to me a defeat, and to kill a person one must surely have an even better reason! No doubt you have thought what killing means — not only to the killer but to the person killed? Forgive me if I say that you sometimes speak of this young man as if he were a mere object of your feelings — love or hate — and had no life of his own, beyond what you feel about him. However, in any case, since you have felt so much about him — even though, you now feel, so mistakenly — you must have been his debtor for a great deal of joy! You would not, therefore, I suppose, willingly cause him excruciating agonies of useless pain? Natural death is generally — though by no means always — painless; but even quite quick killings are always a painful business. Before inflicting even an easy form of death, I should strongly advise anyone to realize what he is inflicting. Women murderers, as a rule, use poison rather than violence. Probably this is because women are less expert than men in the use of weapons, as well as less strong. They prefer therefore to use a thing that does their work for them. But, of course, poisons, with the exception of narcotics, are all exceptionally cruel deaths."

Dr. Silla paused, to take out another cigarette and light it. She had only smoked one since breakfast, and she meant this to be her last; but after she had lit it, she left the subject of sudden death to Hilda.

"A disease isn't exactly a poison, is it?" Hilda asked, in a low voice, after rather a long pause, as if she had hoped that Dr. Silla would go on. "I mean, you get unconscious fairly soon – I thought – people always do get unconscious, when pain is very bad, don't they?"

"In the end they do," Dr. Silla admitted, "but you have to go to the extreme of your powers of endurance, whatever these may happen to be, before you reach unconsciousness. I have known people to die of pain. I should not recommend a kind-hearted person to choose this as a form of murder. As far as that goes, I should not recommend any kind-hearted person to attempt murder at all; nor I think, if such a person had kindness, would he attempt it! Murderers are people who have no social interest."

Hilda sat up with a jerk. "What do you mean by social interest?" she demanded.

"Those who possess it seldom ask the question," Dr. Silla answered, with a faintly ironic smile. "As near as I can define it for you, it is the love of your neighbour."

"Then you think I haven't got any?" Hilda asked

indignantly. "Even though I am doing this awful thing, at the risk of my own life, for Annie?"

Dr. Silla was silent for quite a long time. She looked, Hilda thought, a little ashamed, though whether of having roused such a question – or of the questioner for asking it – Hilda could not quite determine.

At last Dr. Silla threw away her cigarette, and said firmly: "I must tell you, Hilda, that I do not think that you *were* going to commit this murder because you loved your sister – but because you could not bear her to be loved as you had been – by Ronnie. I think from what you have told me, and from what I myself have gathered about you, that you never really loved Ronnie for himself, nor are you hating him for himself now! Few people have learned to love in such a friendly and unselfish fashion! First love is in itself very deceptive; it is so rapturous and inconclusive a business that it seems often to act without any incentive from the lovers themselves. But to love another human being as a desired object – and not for himself – is not real love at all! And when you lose your desired object, you are like a miser robbed of all his gold. You see, I am sorry to put it like this, but it is the truth! You have loved like a miser, and a miser is always a certain temptation to a thief. Also a man or woman cannot bear for long to be hoarded like gold."

Hilda felt as if she were being burned alive, but the fire was within herself and she could not escape it.

"I – I am like a miser?" she stammered. Hitherto she had always thought of herself as an exceptionally generous person.

Dr. Silla made no answer.

After what seemed an eternity at the stake, Hilda got up. She stood in front of Dr. Silla, with her back to the tennis-court and its parrot-cries. "Look here," she said breathlessly, in a voice barely above a whisper, "will you – will you do something for me? I've got something here – in this bag! Something that I want destroyed – but it's dangerous! I don't know how to destroy it! It's tubes with germs in them. Will you – will you throw them away, where they can't do anybody any harm?"

"Do they belong to you?" Dr. Silla asked, driving Hilda frantic by the lucid irrelevance of her question.

"I took them!" Hilda exclaimed. "Can't you guess – I took them from the Laboratory! I pretended to be you – they expected *you* – and *I* went! That's why I didn't post the letter. But they haven't found out. It's all right! They never will now – and they're here! Just as they were! I haven't used them!"

"They are not yours then – either to give to me, or to destroy?" Dr. Silla asked with unhurried calm. "I will not, therefore, undertake to destroy them; but this does not greatly matter. What matters is – since you have offered them to me for that purpose, you must have given up the idea of killing your friend. I am right, am I not, in supposing this?"

"Oh, if you call it right," Hilda said angrily. "You've been speaking all the morning as if I were to blame for everything! And as if Ronnie hadn't done me any harm! Well, now I've given up the idea of killing him – doesn't even *that* satisfy you?"

Dr. Silla made no answer, and Hilda went on, with a rush, pouring out a list of Ronnie's cruelties.

It was a long list, and wound up with what Ronnie had made her Aunt Edith think of her. "If he had even left the past alone," Hilda finished fiercely, "I *might* have forgiven him!"

Dr. Silla listened attentively to the whole story without an interruption. When Hilda stopped speaking, she murmured: "It seems to me that you put too much value upon what Ronnie said to your aunt. It was not true; therefore it had no value. In the long run even your aunt would have realized that it was not true. What does it matter what such a young man says – or even what others ignorantly believe of you? But what you have *done* matters! You asked me, just now, if I did not appreciate the harm Ronnie had done you! I did not answer you – because I wished to hear first what harm you thought he had done you; and now I have listened, and I do not think he did you very much harm. I do not think it was within his power to do so! You have harmed yourself, perhaps, by the way you have taken him; but that is your own affair. Not Ronnie's! He has also very much, I should imagine, harmed himself by the way he has taken you! You are not to blame for that either. Had you wished to do him, or yourself, good, you would of course have acted quite differently, but you do not need me to point this out to you."

"No!" said Hilda defiantly, "I don't! But I think you might at least destroy the tubes – you don't seem to *want* to help me!"

Dr. Silla shook her head. "I have far too much respect for you, to wish to help you, but I have the hope that though you will very much dislike a suggestion I am about to make, you may think it over, and see its reasonableness. I am going to ask you to give those tubes back to the person to whom they belong. No! Do not be afraid. He is already your friend; and no one beside him will ever know, or *should* ever know, what you did!

"Dr. Laing knows that you have taken the tubes; naturally he was alarmed at their disappearance, since he was responsible for them – and rang me up, half an hour after you left the Laboratory. I was able, however, to reassure him. I think it is to him that you should restore them, and he is coming here this afternoon. But I must tell you also that it is within my power to give them back, – if you refuse to see him, – since he had sufficient confidence in me to leave the matter in my hands. I do not know if you have an equal confidence in me or not – I mean the confidence to see him, at my suggestion?"

Hilda turned away, she began to walk towards the gate of the hotel garden; both Dr. Silla and Archer accompanied her in silence. For a time Hilda felt too angry, and too confused, to speak; but after a time this welter of anger and confusion died down in her, and she said at last:

"I can't think why you ask this of me! Why can't you take the tubes and destroy them? You're a doctor – you know how! It will almost kill me to see Dr. Laing again! Don't you see, if he knows, what he must think of me? Haven't I been humiliated enough – first by Ronnie – and now by you? Must I be torn to pieces again before this young man — who at least *once* thought of me with kindness?"

"And whom you fooled for having done so!" Dr. Silla remarked with a dry chuckle. "No, Hilda, you needn't! Give me the tubes. I'll destroy them now. I only thought you might feel that you owed the young man something. You see, though he had done you no harm, you gave him the worst time of any of us — you could have destroyed a township with the contents of those tubes — and he was responsible for leaving you alone in the Laboratory. Suppose you were a homicidal maniac, with just such a purpose! He risked the death of hundreds — and his job into the bargain! I also risked something — first my reputation as a courteous colleague — and, possibly, a trial for murder! No, I am not exaggerating! It is in order that you may not exaggerate that I have asked you to see Dr. Laing this afternoon; because I am certain that he will show you, without even entering upon the subject, that although you have made a great mistake, you have not forfeited either his respect or his sympathy — any more than you have forfeited mine. I even took the liberty of stretching the truth a little — to tell him that you followed this unfortunate impulse in order to save your sister! Perhaps this was not altogether false — for I believe that you *did* very much want to save your sister, though not, I think, so much as you wanted to punish Ronnie for daring to love her instead of you!"

They stood together quite near to the edge of the cliff. There was no more mist left – the whole azure sunny day spread itself out before them.

"I thought," Hilda said in a queer stifled voice, "that you – I mean Annie – " She turned suddenly away from the cliff. "I did not want Ronnie to love anyone else but me," she admitted. "I will give Dr. Laing back the tubes myself, though I wish you hadn't asked me to. But I see they do belong to him – and I *think* I see what you mean, that I *ought* to give them back to him! I want to go for a walk now. When must I be back to meet him? I don't want any lunch!"

Dr. Silla hesitated. Hilda still had the tubes in the bag she was carrying. Suddenly Dr. Silla smiled; holding out her hand to Hilda, she gave her a firm, warm grip, as if she wanted to leave something of herself with Hilda.

"Four o'clock will do very nicely for you to come back," she said, turning briskly back towards the hotel. "The young man should be here by then."

Chapter 16

HILDA walked swiftly for nearly an hour, Archer trotting more or less docilely behind or in front of her; but still the anger seething within her had not even begun to die down.

It ran through her like a consuming fire; but it was anger with herself now; not with Ronnie; not even with Dr. Silla, who had shown Hilda what she was really like. It was funny, Hilda thought, to see herself as wrong where she had felt so certain that she was right! Not about murdering Ronnie, that had always seemed to Hilda a necessity rather than a virtue; but quite definitely and plainly wrong about not posting Dr. Silla's letter for instance; about risking that rather nice young doctor's whole reputation; about giving Annie no choice; and worse still, if there could be worse behind this astonishing list, wrong as she had never yet conceived it possible that she might be wrong — in her actual relationship with Ronnie. Was it really power over Ronnie that she had loved better than Ronnie; and was it giving up this power to Annie that she minded more than poor little Annie's future sufferings? Where was the point at issue that had seemed so crystal-clear to her before? After all, when Hilda came right down to it, Annie hadn't *wanted* Ronnie killed in order that she mightn't have to suffer. This was such a curious idea that Hilda actually stood stock-still in the middle of a country lane, in order to clear her mind. What may have helped to clear it was a sign-post pointing straight ahead — a quarter of a mile to Baresfrere.

This was where Alice Amondson, the "Hag Beauty," lived; and where Ronnie was no doubt staying.

Wherever one went to get away from Ronnie, Hilda thought irritably, one was always fated to run up against him; whereas when you really wanted him, he could have given an eel points in evasiveness. He might have already gone back to town puffed up with his easy victory over Aunt Edith. However she'd better be careful, and turn back before she actually struck the village. Suddenly, round a blind corner, with a silent swishing speed, filling up all the lane, a big Daimler was upon them. Hilda heard the shriek of the brake, and watched spellbound the heedless little white body of Archer dive under the front of the car; then with a bare flicker of a pause, Hilda dived after him; but only the mudguard caught her, and flung her, bruised but safe, against the hedge.

"My God — did I get you?" shouted the agitated motorist, and — seeing that he hadn't, in any serious sense, "got" Hilda, and being in a hurry — tore relentlessly on.

Hilda was alone on the dusty roadside, with the twitching, strangely silent body of Archer. She picked it up, while the blood poured over her Sunday dress. She had never felt alone like this before, as if the world had emptied itself of friendliness and aid. The sun shone pitilessly upon them with a kind of derisive spite. Archer's light body felt heavy in her arms. Hilda remembered how he had always made his body feel heavy when he was being carried in any direction that he wished to avoid.

For a moment or two, staring down at his body, Hilda had a confused feeling, as if she had, after all, killed Ronnie.

She must get help from somewhere, she told herself, and Baresfrere was the nearest place; so, carrying

Archer in her arms, she walked on rather stiffly.

She couldn't see how beautiful the tiny yellow stone village was, lying deep between high hedges, and long sloping golden fields. She looked at the names on the gateways; and, opposite a tiny church that you might have put under a thimble and that time had kept incredibly solid and serene, Hilda saw "Spillfeathers" written on a white post; with hollyhocks leading up to an open doorway, and a tall woman leaning over the gate. The woman didn't give her time to explain, she simply opened the gate, and drew Hilda and Archer straight into the avenue of crimson and salmon-pink hollyhocks.

She was a worn-looking woman with deep sapphire-coloured eyes, and a strong patient expression. There didn't seem anyone else about; and Hilda soon found herself sitting in a garden chair, while Mrs. Amondson telephoned for a vet, and Archer twitched himself quieter and quieter on Hilda's knees. Mrs. Amondson brought Hilda out a liqueur glass of neat brandy, and Hilda said "Oh no!"; drank it; choked; and felt better.

"It's a great pity that a young friend we have staying with us has taken my two-seater out for the afternoon," Mrs. Amondson told Hilda, "but the vet's a dear, and he'll take you in his car wherever you want.

Your dress is spoilt – can't I lend you something?"
Hilda thanked her, and shook her head. She had begun to tremble all over, because Archer had stopped twitching; he gave a little sigh and lay quite still; and Hilda suddenly wanted to say "No!" to everything.

"I'm going back to a friend's to tea – if the vet'll take me," she forced herself to say at last, "and then I'll have to tell my aunt. It's her dog; and that makes it much worse, of course. You see, I didn't have him on the lead – I wasn't thinking about him properly."

"I'm quite sure it wasn't your fault," Mrs. Amondson said firmly. "You mustn't think it was; it makes things so much worse always. The lane is very narrow, and the corner's blind; no car should have come fast round it, but they often do."

Hilda looked at her, at the worn, time-sculptured face and greying hair. Was it possible that Ronnie should have written all that wicked rubbish to her? But perhaps she liked it, just because she'd had too much to be patient about!

It was true that she still had a sort of beauty, but she hadn't bothered about it, and you would have expected – since Ronnie had taken a fancy to her – that she would have *had* to bother. She was dressed all wrong too, in nothing particular, and had been working in the garden. She was probably poor; and yet not very poor either, or surely Ronnie would not have been staying with her? Hilda hesitated; should she tell Mrs. Amondson who she was? But then Mrs. Amondson would despise her! She didn't want those straightforward sapphire eyes to lose their pity and their kindness.

If Hilda just said "I'm that girl you advised Ronnie to break with. It's all right – I *am* broken!" Mrs. Amondson might think that she'd come tagging round after Ronnie again, and despise her still more.

On the other hand there was the chance of really showing up Ronnie; and this was the kind of rather shy, rather decent fair-minded woman who could be counted on to recognize the truth if it were put straight to her.

Hilda knew that if she said: "Look here, one doesn't get a dog run over on purpose, does one? If I hadn't needed help, I'd never have come near the place; but now I *am* here, and Archer is dead, I might as well tell you that I meant to kill Ronnie too, but not for nothing! I don't like killing things! It was because Ronnie was cruel and mean, not only to me, but to my little Annie and to you too – if you only knew it – and to his mother, who's a friend of yours. Why should he call her a 'Cormorant'? She loves him, doesn't she! And she doesn't *know* she's being called a 'Cormorant'; that's what I mind: He's fooling all of us all round – it isn't only my wanting power over him! He laughs at *you* behind your back – just as he laughed at me – just as he will laugh at Annie!"

The words came to the tip of Hilda's tongue; they seemed in some curious way to have even got off it into the garden, and to be as much a part of it as the jewelled roses – apricot; bronze; coral; cream and carmine, that spilt themselves between her and the neat-cropped velvet lawn. But none of the words *did* get off the tip of Hilda's tongue after all.

"Have you a husband?" she heard herself asking instead, in a half-witted sort of way.

"Yes," the Hag Beauty answered, without any shamed hesitation, in the confronting fact, in spite of Ronnie. "He was very badly injured in the War; and he has not got better. He has gone out for a walk with the vicar; but he will be back in time for tea."

"He mustn't see this blood on my dress then," Hilda said hoarsely. "It might remind him of the War!"

"It's kind of you to think of that," the Hag Beauty said more gently still, "but he won't see it – he is blind. He likes his Sunday walks with the vicar very much. Our vicar is so kind – people are, in villages, I think. You saw our church perhaps, just over the way? It's one of the oldest and smallest in England."

"Yes," Hilda admitted, "I saw it." Had this woman deceived her husband with Ronnie – her blind husband? Were those steady sapphire eyes liars, in that worn sculptured face? What was life really like after all? Or was the whole thing perhaps *not* the way Ronnie had twisted it into being? He'd made it sound so cheap; so ugly; so nasty – but could he make life like that? Wasn't it only something in Ronnie, that didn't make anything at all? Hadn't Hilda perhaps always taken what he'd talked about much too seriously?

"It makes you tremble to see anything killed," Hilda said in explanation for the stupid way her legs kept shaking. "Just to see it, I mean, or anyone hurt awfully, like your husband – it must have hurt *you* like that – but perhaps living with it, you would get used to it – and forget?"

"In a sense you do get used to it," Mrs. Amondson said reflectively; "perhaps too used to it – I mean one can't ever remember *enough*, if one's living with a person who's been desperately injured, what they've lost. If one forgot, it would be no use living with them, would it? They have to trust you to keep remembering it."

Suddenly Hilda felt quite sure that, whatever Ronnie had said, this woman *hadn't* betrayed her husband.

That letter was Ronnie's. It wasn't hers; it wasn't even, in any real sense, *about* her. This woman could only think of Ronnie as a friend, and all that caddishness about Annie and herself – could she ever have swallowed that? It didn't seem likely. Or was she thinking all the while of something else in Ronnie – something finer and better than Hilda had ever seen? Ronnie had never told Hilda that the Hag Beauty's husband was blind; he had said, "She's married of course, to an ass. That doesn't help matters." But supposing the whole thing was one of Ronnie's fairy tales . . . Then he might all the while have been nice to the blind husband – even be perhaps *his* friend as well as *hers;* and there was something about her that made Hilda think her friends would always *have* to be friends of the blind husband too! The woman didn't say anything. She was a very quiet woman, and though she sat quite still, she was long and lean, as if she took a great deal of exercise, and lived almost entirely in the open air.

There was the garden of course. It was, Hilda could see, an extraordinarily perfect small garden. Two long herbaceous borders, with grass paths between them, stretched away on each side of the emerald lawn, and behind them stood sun-soaked yellow stone walls. Sometimes a blackbird gave a long liquid gurgle of delight, and sometimes a thrush ran up and down his eager scale; but except for birds, and the vague hum of bees in lavender bushes, there was no sound at all.

No wonder Ronnie liked being there! But he shouldn't have laughed at her – this woman who had made it all so beautiful! "But it doesn't matter," Hilda said to herself, suddenly angry in a different, more scornful way. "I mean it's *his* look-out – *let* him laugh at her if he likes! Even if she knew perhaps she wouldn't care, because after all she isn't to *be* laughed at!"

"This friend you've got staying with you," Hilda said aloud, "who took out your car – does he help you with your husband? I mean – you must sometimes need help?"

The sapphire eyes that had been resting on the roses came back to Hilda's face with a faintly surprised glance. "Oh no," she said, "not now! I don't think either of us need help now. We used to, those first years – when he was so young; but he has made his life over again now. It's a very good one really. That boy in the car is just the son of a great friend of mine! It's nice of him to come and stay with us sometimes. We have no children of our own. He must find it very dull."

"The Cormorant" was what Ronnie called this woman's friend – his mother. Did Mrs. Amondson call her that too? Did she laugh at her friend, with her friend's son? It didn't sound very likely. Or had Ronnie perhaps meant "the Cormorant" in a playful, loving way? Perhaps he was more playful than Hilda knew – or perhaps this lady only thought he was?

Mrs. Amondson suddenly smiled. "Other people's children," she said, "are very funny sometimes. You see, they take themselves so seriously, while you can't help taking them rather as a joke – I don't mean an unkind joke, but – well, yes – as a joke! Perhaps boys especially, they're so terribly important to themselves, and to their mothers, aren't they? Too important I think sometimes! So they get into the habit!"

"The habit of being important?" Hilda demanded a little breathlessly, because the idea threw rather a new light on Ronnie.

The Hag Beauty nodded. "I think I hear the vet's car," she said, standing up.

It was the vet's car; and the vet, a very kind, rather red-faced young man, in a tight blue Sunday suit, got out of it. There wasn't anything whatever that he could do for Archer, except take charge of his body; but he was very willing to give Hilda a lift back to the Kingsway Hotel. Hilda shook hands with the Hag

Beauty very hard over the garden gate. She knew she wasn't ever going to see her again, but she wished that she could. Hilda felt quite sure of the Hag Beauty now, and curiously glad that she hadn't said to her anything against Ronnie. After all, if Mrs. Amondson could like Ronnie – like him in a laughing, kindly way, as if he wasn't important – why should Hilda take that away from her? Or for the matter of that, take it away from Ronnie either? Hilda knew that she *would* have taken it away, if she had told Mrs. Amondson the truth about Ronnie. Mrs. Amondson wouldn't have laughed at that particular kind of truth. But Dr. Silla had made Hilda feel a little unsure about what the truth really was; and now, having seen Mrs. Amondson, having heard about the blind husband, Hilda began to feel still more uncertain of the truth. Still there was that letter, written to the Hag Beauty by Ronnie! How could you get past that letter?

Suddenly it occurred to Hilda, with an extraordinary flash of conviction, that Ronnie wasn't going to send that letter at all! That was why the flap had never been licked down; and Hilda had found it, tucked away in a pocket. Had he – being Ronnie – written it just for the fun of the thing; and as a new way of getting his knife into Hilda? All that nastiness about herself and Annie, had it never been meant for

Mrs. Amondson's eyes at all – but perhaps only for Hilda's own? He knew that she always brushed his clothes. He knew that she always hung them up properly in his wardrobe! And had he counted that she also went through his pockets? Wives did! Why not mistresses – especially discarded ones! That would account for everything – for what he'd *said* about the Hag Beauty needn't be taken seriously at all – it was all a part of his easy boasting. He liked to think everyone fell for him. And it would have been especially a good joke to have tricked Hilda into being dishonourable enough to read a letter he hadn't the slightest intention of sending!

"My God – Ronnie!" Hilda exclaimed. Why couldn't she have been allowed to comfortably and gently kill him? He'd know too, by her having licked the flap down, that she *had* read the letter; and believed he meant to send it! It was a thousand pities she hadn't stamped and posted it; that would have brought his sins nicely home to him. He wouldn't have been asked to stay at Spillfeathers again, after that letter.

"I wouldn't take it too much to heart if I were you," the red-faced young man burst out earnestly. "Hit too quickly to know what struck him – that's how I look at it! There's many worse deaths than that!"

"Yes," Hilda said, repressing a desire to laugh hysterically, "you're right – there are worse deaths than that. Only they don't always happen, do they, to those who most deserve them?"

The young man agreed that they didn't.

Chapter 17

AS soon as Dr. Silla had heard about the accident she took Hilda straight to her room, and made her change into one of her own dresses. It hung loosely on Hilda, but was otherwise quite effective.

"It isn't the first time you've dressed up to look like me, is it?" Dr. Silla demanded with a twinkle in her eyes; but in spite of her little joke, she managed to make Hilda understand that she really and truly minded about Archer.

"He was a most friendly, intelligent little dog," she said gravely, "and it's hard for you to have to tell your aunt!"

Hilda stared at her with eyes full of the horror she had managed, until now, to hide. "You see," she whispered, "I didn't put him on the lead! I let him run out on to the main road. I was so angry I didn't notice – I didn't care! I had – I had no social interest!"

"Oh, well," said Dr. Silla, with a kindness that was all the more real, because it came into her voice and her eyes, rather than into the words she said. "That poor dog had never learned to look after himself. Sooner or later, something bad was sure to happen to him! As it happens to all spoilt creatures! Are you still angry?" she added, putting her hand a little shyly upon Hilda's arm.

"No," Hilda said, "not now; and I don't mind about meeting Dr. Laing now, either."

"But it isn't only Dr. Laing that you will have to meet," Dr. Silla answered gravely, after a moment's pause. "It's rather odd, and I'm afraid you mayn't like it, but it seems that Ronnie rang up your Aunt Edith to give you a message from me, a message that he had previously told me at your mother's that he wouldn't be able to give.

"It suddenly occurred to him that, being in the neighbourhood, he might as well pass it on through your Aunt Edith – and I suppose earn a little appreciation for his considerateness, from us both. Your aunt, however, to use Mr. Ronnie's expression, was a little 'crisp' with him. She said: 'Please give your own message to my niece. When I last heard of her she was with Dr. Silla at the Kingsway Hotel, but she must have left by now – since she went to breakfast with her, and can hardly have remained with her all day.' So Mr. Ronnie came on here by himself, thinking that you would probably have gone on somewhere else!"

"He must have been bored with the friends he was staying with, to risk meeting me," Hilda said thoughtfully, "or else he's what he calls 'intrigued' with you! He'll put up with anything when he's intrigued!"

"Before this cruel accident," Dr. Silla said gently, "I had not supposed that his being here, on your arrival, would matter very greatly, but now I think you have had enough to bear. Shall I go downstairs and send him away?"

Hilda hesitated. It seemed to her that something rather vital was at stake. She walked to the window, and stood with her back to Dr. Silla, looking out blindly at the pale, peaceful sea. The soft grey dress she had put on gave her a curious calm feeling, as if she had put on more than her friend's clothes, and had acquired a little of her spirit.

"I think I'd rather like to meet Ronnie," she said at last, "with you here. He hasn't made you like him any better, has he?"

Dr. Silla gave a faint sound like a suppressed laugh, but she wasn't even smiling when Hilda turned round and looked at her.

"There has been nothing to make me change my opinion of Mr. Ronnie," she replied, "but it certainly interests me to see how hard he tries to win approval. He must have very little confidence in himself to have to work so hard to earn it from others! Dr. Laing doesn't like him – but that, I suppose, was to be expected. Shall we go down to tea?"

Hilda asked "Why shouldn't Dr. Laing like Ronnie?" as they went downstairs.

Dr. Silla really laughed now. She said: "Well, if you don't know the answer to that question – how should I?"

Did Dr. Silla mean that Dr. Laing wouldn't like Ronnie because of Hilda?

That was a flattering thought, and for a moment it brought the colour into Hilda's cheeks; but could Dr. Silla have meant that? Dr. Laing knew that Hilda had meant to be a murderess – he couldn't care what she thought of any young man after that. He must despise her; and yet, as Hilda crossed the hall, beside Dr. Silla's straight, solid figure, she found that she was holding her head higher than usual, as if she had got over her reason for feeling despised.

The tea-table was set out in the lounge, by an open window. Through the window sand blew into the jam; and in the lounge itself the inferior cigarette smoke of the past week poisoned the air.

In the far corner of the lounge, a little group of earnest young people were talking about religion. They were talking rather loud, as if they wished their voices to carry, so that Hilda could not help overhearing what they said. Apparently they managed life better than most people, and were in hourly contact with a Deity who played into their hands.

Dr. Silla, after she had explained about Archer's accident in a few non-conducting words, sat at the head of the table with Ronnie on one side of her, and Adrian Laing on the other. Hilda sat on the further side of Adrian.

Hilda had seen at a glance, when they joined the two men, that the only subject Ronnie and Adrian Laing would ever have in common was their intense dislike of each other.

When they spoke to each other at all, they dropped ice into their voices and blocked each other's topics.

Dr. Silla never had any small talk; she merely saw that everybody had what they could get to eat on an English Sunday afternoon, and marvelled in silence that it was not more attractive.

Hilda, her whole body and mind vibrating with the shock of Archer's death, was quite unable either to eat or to lighten the social atmosphere.

After a minute or two of sympathetic condolence about Archer, Ronnie turned his shoulder upon Laing and Hilda, and devoted his whole attention, scintillating like a diamond, upon the pleasant but hitherto undazzled figure of Dr. Silla.

After Ronnie was thoroughly launched, Dr. Laing said in a low voice to Hilda: "It was good of you to meet me. Will you let me drive you back to wherever you live? I came in my car."

"Yes," Hilda agreed, "that would be best." She had not wanted to meet him, but now that he was actually there beside her, with his grave, young eyes bent on hers in shy kindness, Hilda felt a vague sense of relief. He was not, she could see, disgusted with her, nor was he trying to be good to her. He simply *was* good, in a merciful, impersonal way, without bothering to be superior about it. On the way back in his car would do very well for returning the tubes to him.

Perhaps Dr. Silla had been right not to take over the poison herself and destroy it. If she had done that Hilda would never really have felt safe. She would have been haunted by the fear of suddenly running across Adrian Laing in a bus or a tube, and reading in his startled eyes that he thought her a murderer.

This could not happen now, because for some reason or other, without the smart of pity, Adrian had let her off being a murderer. He simply thought she had had a bad time, and made a muddle of it; and he saw, or else he had felt by instinct, that Ronnie was the excusable cause of her bad time.

But however nice Adrian was, Hilda could not talk to him; the image of Archer and the accident held her senses, with the rawness of an open wound. She could not get past the accident still happening in her mind, into the outer world.

At last Adrian said to her, in a voice so low that the others could not hear him: "I know about dogs, I have one myself – don't bother to talk, just go on drinking your tea."

If Hilda had been alone with Adrian, or with Dr. Silla and Adrian, she might have gone on drinking her tea, until she felt better. She might even have been able to talk to them about the accident, and that would have slowed down the recurrent image of it; but Ronnie's voice, caressing, tender, Ronnie's being so amusing and witty on the top of it all, was more than Hilda could bear.

Once more she felt anger coursing through her veins like fire.

A few hours ago Hilda (under the new, unendurable light of her own complicity) had felt prepared to accept Ronnie's faults and their results without condemnation, but she had not had Ronnie under her eyes at the time, scraping against her smarting senses with his callousness. Ronnie rollicking in her defeat; Ronnie unable to forbear, in the midst of what he thought was his new conquest, casting a triumphant glance in Hilda's direction to see how she took it . . . Ronnie, thinking, and glorying in the thought, that Hilda's inability to talk to Adrian was a tribute to his own charm. She could not, poor submerged creature, his cruelly pleased eyes told her, *not* listen to him, if he talked, although not one word of it was meant for her.

This would go on, and go on worse than ever, at Rostrevor Road. Hilda was not deceived by Dr. Silla's tolerant amusement. She knew that her new friend had not fallen a victim to Ronnie's charm; but Annie, and even in a lesser way her mother and father, were Ronnie's willing victims. She would have to go back into this circle of defeat, with no way out of it; and with her new knowledge of her partial responsibility for it making her burden, for the moment, even harder to bear.

It was all very well for those earnest young people

in the corner to talk about God and His playful rescues. One of them was just telling the others how God had helped her to have a holiday, although she had spent all her holiday money on a sick friend, who, in answer to prayer, made a brisk recovery.

That was not the kind of thing God did for Hilda. Hilda's sick friend would have died; the holiday money have been wasted; and Hilda would not have had the holiday. For God did these things too. He had not saved Abyssinia, Spain, China, or Austria from being set upon by Imperial gangsters.

Someone had once told Hilda: "Surgeons forget their failures." So apparently did God and His disciples.

It was all very well for Dr. Silla to imagine that by thinking less of Ronnie, and more of herself, Hilda might not mind what Ronnie was up to; but when it came to Ronnie's spoiling Annie's life as well as her own, Hilda *did* mind it! And she minded more, now that she had not got the poison to fall back upon. But she still had it!

Suddenly Hilda sat up straight, and looked across the table at Ronnie. Something might still be done with those tubes in her bag.

She lifted it from her lap to the table. It was a very pretty bag, given her the Christmas before by Ronnie. She unfastened the tiny sparkling clasp with a click. Ronnie turned his head and met her summoning eyes.

Out of the bag Hilda drew the carefully packed tubes, and laid them on the table in front of Adrian's plate.

She spoke, so that Ronnie and Dr. Silla would have to listen to her, though not so loud as to be heard by the religious young people in the corner.

"Dr. Laing," Hilda said with bitter resentment, "here are the tubes of the Shiga bacilli that I took from your Laboratory. I meant to kill Ronnie with them; but you see I haven't done it. I'm sorry I took them, because I shouldn't have given you such a fright or upset Dr. Silla's plans; but otherwise, as far as Ronnie is concerned, I'm *not* sorry." It was a pity perhaps to break down the confidence between herself and her new friends; but it was her only weapon against Ronnie. If she was not going to kill Ronnie, she might at least frighten him off his course. She watched Ronnie's eyes turn from incredulity to horror, and from horror to abject fear. He shrank back in his chair like an old, old man; but his face had a still greater helplessness — the helplessness of a frightened child.

"She's mad! She's mad! She's dangerous! Take her

away!" he whispered, turning his helpless eyes on Dr. Silla's strong, expressionless face.

Dr. Laing took the tubes, and slipped them into his pocket, in a matter-of-course way that was extraordinarily reassuring to Hilda; then he looked at her, with eyes that had a positive twinkle in them, as if he were amused, or even rather pleased, by this sudden overthrow of all public decency. But Hilda was not so sure of Dr. Silla – there was no approval in the level gaze that met her own across the dull, half-eaten meal.

"There is no danger at all now," Dr. Silla said quietly, but although she spoke to Ronnie, she looked at Hilda, "for anybody, that is to say, except Hilda."

Hilda sprang to her feet, and Dr. Silla too rose, though more slowly; they walked away from the table side by side, past the earnest group, who suddenly stopped talking as they reached them, appalled by something more real, on these two set faces, than anything in their neatly survived ordeals.

Dr. Silla and Hilda walked up the shallow stairs, stiffly and in silence, to Dr. Silla's room. As, after they had reached it, Dr. Silla still said nothing, Hilda began changing her dress. The silence went on and on, and seemed to become heavier and heavier.

At last Hilda herself broke it. "What do you mean," she demanded fiercely, "by danger to me? and *not* to anybody else? What danger? I've given back the tubes, haven't I?"

Dr. Silla stood with her back turned to Hilda, looking out of the window on the tennis-court. "You're still angry," she said without turning round. "Don't you remember telling me: 'I was so angry that I forgot to put on Archer's lead!' "

"Oh, don't – don't *tell* me that!" Hilda cried out in anguish. "I can't bear it! I can't bear it! I *did* forget his lead!"

"Then you must know that anger is dangerous," Dr. Silla said inexorably. "You *helped* to kill Archer, didn't you? Why should you punish Ronnie for it? Don't you see that by using force to try to prevent what may happen in the future, you are only damaging yourself? Don't you see that as long as you will try to use force upon other people's concerns, the material you are using will react upon yourself? You will not help them by the use of anger. You think *now* that you have helped your sister – and I admit Ronnie may give her up from fear of what you might still do to him – but will that make your sister, who needs your love, able to believe in it? You have probably done her more harm than good already – for she believes now in Ronnie, who is not trustworthy, rather than in you, who are, as far as she is concerned, fit to be trusted. And what have you done to Ronnie? Because he hadn't the courage to stand up to you? I will tell you something that I believe you have not seen for yourself. I believe Ronnie would love you still – only he doesn't dare! You've taken away more and more of his courage! Just now you took away almost all he had!"

Hilda let Dr. Silla's loose dress fall to the floor. She stood quite still, staring down at it, lying in a little pool of grey tussore silk, round her feet; it was a soft, strong silk, without stiffness. At last she raised her head and said hardly above a whisper: "I can't help it! It was so horrible! Why did he talk like that to you? Why must he always show off? Why is he in love with himself? I could love him if he weren't! but I don't! I know what you mean, about his still loving me – he has to notice me if I'm there, if it's only to show off before me; in that sense perhaps he *does* still love me! He'd like me to go on adoring him – if you call that love! But it wouldn't do him any good. When I *did* adore him it did him nothing but harm, you said so yourself!"

"It *would* do him nothing but harm being adored," Dr. Silla agreed, "but, Hilda, suppose you had respected Ronnie instead of adoring him? That would have done him no harm!"

"What is there to respect in him?" Hilda demanded irritably. "*You* don't respect him yourself, though you *behave* as if you do!"

"Oh, yes," Dr. Silla said quietly, "I do respect Ronnie as a fellow human being with the rights of a fellow human being. You allow him no such rights; so that you have roused in him no feeling that could help him to respect himself. That is his trouble, he acts very basely because he thinks he must act basely to succeed at all. He has a right to wish for success and to mind defeats, as great as any right of your own; but he has not the confidence to look for success in the right direction; nor have you helped him to find it."

Hilda picked up her own lilac linen dress, it looked very nice against the dark red of her hair, but she dragged it on mercilessly, and did not look at herself in the glass, when she had finished.

"I'm ready now," she said briefly; then she stooped down and picked up Dr. Silla's grey tussore silk, and put it carefully over the edge of the bed. "I've finished! I suppose you hate me? I don't expect I shall ever see you again!"

"That depends on yourself," Dr. Silla told Hilda.

"I shall send you my address and even if we don't meet again, I shall always be your friend."

"My friend?" Hilda exclaimed astonished. "Why – don't you despise me?"

"Have I acted as if I despised you?" Dr. Silla asked her. "And haven't I acted as if I were your friend? If I despised you, I should be your enemy; I do not think that I have acted like an enemy."

"No," Hilda said slowly, "you haven't! I hadn't thought of that! Well, according to that point of view, I suppose you're the best friend I ever had – except Mums."

Dr. Silla smiled. "It seems to me that you always exaggerate," she said, "but in this direction it is better than the other. Certainly I will be as good a friend to you as I can!"

They walked downstairs in such a different silence that Hilda could have laughed aloud. She felt quite free, and even that harsh agony of the accident no longer danced before her eyes.

Ronnie carefully turned away from Hilda as they joined him in the hall; he asked, with an air of injured dignity, if he might have a few moments with Dr. Silla, alone. She said "Of course," and looked at Hilda. Suddenly Hilda found herself in Dr. Silla's arms. Dr. Silla kissed her warmly, first on one cheek and then on the other, while Ronnie stood looking on aghast. He was almost sorry that he had asked to stay, for surely this was another madwoman, kissing a murderer as if she loved her!

But after all, he reassured himself by thinking, he *was* staying behind and might soon be counted on to change Dr. Silla's too optimistic opinion of Hilda.

Hilda passed Ronnie with her head held high; without so much as a glance at him. She went straight out of the lounge door, to where that wooden young idiot of a laboratory assistant was waiting with his car. They drove off together without once looking back.

"Well," Ronnie murmured in a low voice to his half-finished conquest, who was standing by him in silence, "I suppose she'll start trying to murder *that* young booby next! Thank God *I've* got away from her now, at any rate!"

Dr. Silla returned Ronnie's admiring glance with a curious, speculative look; then she said, rather too professionally, Ronnie thought: "Shall we sit down, and have our talk together here, or would you prefer to go into the garden?"

Chapter 18

RONNIE felt as if he were sinking into something ineffably warm and safe; Dr. Silla's soothing presence was like what he had fondly imagined in his childhood the substance of a fleecy cloud might be: at once soft and firm.

Side by side they sat and smoked; the sea air played pleasantly about them, the voices of the soul-hunters in the distance rose and fell, as a fountain rises and falls, in the exciting spray of their experiences.

The light of the late summer afternoon withdrew itself slowly across the golden patch of lawn.

The shock of Hilda's brutal revelation had stripped bare Ronnie's every nerve, but the friendly silence of this strange woman wrapt each raw filament in a new peace.

Had she been a man, or even a woman like a man, Ronnie would not have felt so quickly appeased, but this foreign woman had a velvety friendliness against which his shivering spirit felt supported. She was not going to bother him with sex because she was not bothered with it herself; on the contrary her sex was a pleasure to her, and she used it as a pleasure.

She was not afraid of this particular instinct, as most Englishwomen are, nor did she use it with the overemphasis of bravado. Dr. Silla simply gave Ronnie the impression that unless he annoyed her as a human being, he was certain to please her as a man, and that taking for granted he would *not* annoy her, she would certainly try to please him as a woman.

Since he was fond of cats, Ronnie compared her in his mind with a beautifully large, soft, plum-coloured cat; but she was perhaps even more like a ripe apricot.

He drew a slow long breath of relief, and then leaning towards her, half smiling, half frowning, he murmured: "What a horrible experience! Do you think Hilda's sane? and do you really think she won't somehow or other contrive to attack me again?"

Dr. Silla drew her golden eyebrows slightly together. "Sane, but angry," she answered gravely, "very, very angry. Can you give me any idea of why she should be so angry with you?"

Ronnie hesitated; after all this warm and pleasant woman had also (in her farewell at least) been warm and pleasant to Hilda. She must know Hilda too, better than she knew Ronnie, though it did not follow that she liked her nearly as well. Still, presumably, they had had several conversations together, and it was even possible (though barely probable) that Hilda had told her their whole story. She might even have admitted that she had taken those frightful tubes to revenge herself upon him, though surely, in that case, Dr. Silla would have handed her over to the police?

Ronnie started shivering again, when he remembered what Hilda had intended to do with the contents of those little tubes. "Hasn't Hilda given you *her* version of our little affair already?" he asked Dr. Silla cautiously.

"Angry people do not always know what has caused their anger," Dr. Silla promptly answered. "In order to understand the real history of a quarrel you must always hear both sides, and if possible you should also know both parties to the quarrel, though sometimes, it is true, one is enough. You asked me a second question also, did you not? You asked if I thought you in any further danger from Hilda. You asked me this question twice. Will you not let me know on what you based it? Did you yourself think you had in any way wronged her?"

"All right – I'll tell you!" Ronnie agreed, drawing a still deeper breath of relief, before he plunged into his side of the story. It was, after all, exactly what he most wanted to do. He wanted reassurance from this new force beside him; he was still shocked and terrified by Hilda's horrible threat. He wanted to feel sure that he was safe from Hilda, and he also wanted as much, if not more, to escape from a half-blind agonizing fear that he had earned Hilda's revenge.

There was still that scent of danger in the air.

Hilda had not acted like a defeated person. Why had she driven off with a smile upon her lips; and her head held as high as before he had discarded her?

If Hilda wanted to kill him, Ronnie knew her well enough to suppose that she would not easily give up the idea. Obviously she had been checked in her poisoning attempt, or else had shrunk in time from its slow cruelty. She was no cat-and-mouse woman. If she no longer meant to kill him, then that smile meant something more dreadful still; it meant that she did not think it worth her while to kill him. To mortally wound his vanity was, to Ronnie, as fatal a disaster as physical death.

He felt that he must at all costs reconstitute himself a conqueror in his own eyes; and if possible in Dr. Silla's. But he fully realized that in painting his former relations with Hilda, he would have to be more careful than usual. He had better not try to make Dr. Silla believe that Hilda had forced herself upon him and that he had yielded unwillingly to her solicitations, in a moment of masculine weakness. Probably Dr. Silla would know that masculine weakness does not often act unwillingly. She might even guess that Hilda was not the sort of girl to attack the virtue of resistant males.

It would be safer, while still staging himself as Hilda's victim, to take a slightly more robust and sophisticated line.

Ronnie, therefore, began to paint himself before the attentive gaze of Dr. Silla not as a lover, but as a man of the world; a man who only wanted a little love, and did not want that little, long. He had, Ronnie explained, supposed himself to be met by an equally initiated and light-hearted girl. The staggering earnestness of first love was not at all what he had bargained for. Hilda's intelligence had taken him in.

He was horrified to find out that at twenty-five she had had no sex experience.

"English girls take chastity very seriously still," Dr.

Silla reminded Ronnie, but not reproachfully, merely as if she were recalling a not unimportant point to his notice. "It has a value to them, I find, even apart from their inclinations."

"Well, yes, with some of them, I admit it has," Ronnie handsomely acknowledged. "But really in the sort of set I move in, it's fifty-fifty! Half of the girls I know would take you on like winking, and naturally one knows enough not to bother about the other half. Hilda apparently belonged to the more intelligent type. Her trouble was – not to put too fine a point upon it – class! Hilda is typically bourgeois. I had overlooked that fact."

Ronnie paused for a moment, to light Dr. Silla and himself fresh cigarettes. He thought her mouth very beautiful as he approached it; and well painted. She let him approach it as closely as he liked, but withdrew her head, without brusquerie, at the exact moment that her cigarette was well alight.

"And the sister," she asked slightly fluttering her long golden eyelashes, "is she also bourgeois?"

It was rather a good thing, Ronnie thought to himself, to have found out that Dr. Silla knew about Annie before he had made a break.

It would never have done, since she *did* know about

her, to have avoided, as he had intended to avoid, all mention of Annie's existence.

"I was just coming to Annie," he said quickly. "No, she isn't exactly bourgeois, she's a pretty little flirt; and flirts are the same, aren't they, whatever class they happen to be born in?"

"As a psychologist," Dr. Silla said (but rather humbly, as if to be a psychologist was perhaps a limitation), "I am not accustomed to consider types. My school of psychology being Adlerian, I believe that people are as individual as their fingerprints."

"Well, of course I know what you mean," Ronnie, who did not know in the least what she meant, hastened to assert. "But Annie, you know, is rather a type! She's the sort of girl who will go as far as she wants to without much fuss. I dare say she won't go any further. You may be surprised to hear that I really haven't tried to find out how far she *might* be willing to go! I'm not, however, the Don Juan type, I merely fell back on Annie as an immense relief after Hilda. It was unfortunate, I am willing to admit, that they happened to be sisters and live under the same roof. But after all, Hilda and I never meet now, and Annie and I meet as much as possible – elsewhere! If I had left the house before (now, of course, I *shall* leave *immediately*) it would, I knew, have thrown out the family exchequer! As a matter of fact Hilda's mother is a dear old thing, as you must have seen for yourself the other day, and I'm really fond of her, that is the reason I *didn't* leave before! But, of course, that doesn't hold good now; I shall send a friend of mine to-morrow, to get my things, and clear out at once."

The eyes that looked into his own flickered for a moment, but they did not express Dr. Silla's thought, they only continued to express her full attention.

"This affair of yours with the elder sister, then," she asked reflectively, "had it come to an end before you met the younger one?"

Ronnie hesitated once more; still it was hardly a question here of how much Dr. Silla knew, it was much more a question of whom she decided to believe; supposing that Ronnie chose to lie, she had only Hilda's word against his.

"*Practically* at an end," Ronnie compromised with the rigour of fact sufficiently to admit. "I was through before, really, if Hilda had had the sense to see it; but she's one of those girls who go on holding on, when there's nothing to hold on to – if you know what I mean?"

The long golden lashes flickered again. Dr. Silla knew what Ronnie meant.

It was really wonderful, for a foreigner, how well she understood colloquial English.

"This question of class," she took up, after a slight pause, "it plays a great part with you here in England then, does it?"

"In a sense it does," Ronnie agreed, "the better class you are, the more you know a thing or two about life, and therefore the more easily you take things! Pluck – restraint – *savoir faire* – that's what one expects to find, and generally *does* find, in a girl of one's own class. They take what's coming to them; and if they don't like it – well, they consume their own smoke, and that rather tends to keep everything in the garden lovely, doesn't it?"

Dr. Silla's English was not, perhaps, quite equal to this last speech, but Ronnie thought, from the neat little nod she gave, after she had carefully stubbed her cigarette out on the ash-tray between them, that she had caught the gist of what he meant.

"You ask me if you are safe," Dr. Silla then demanded, sitting up suddenly rather straight, and looking at Ronnie with extreme earnestness. "I think I ought to tell you, Mr. Ronnie, that I think you are in very great danger!"

Ronnie gave a start of surprise, and not only of surprise: Once more he was frightened to the roots of his being. "But I thought you said," he stammered, "that – that Hilda was not dangerous any more?"

"Hilda is not," Dr. Silla agreed. "That is to say, that I doubt very much if she will ever think of killing you again, although I think you are perhaps wise to seek another lodging. To see that dog killed was enough to show Hilda her mistake. Such an experience is a great help to one's sense of reality. But you, Mr. Ronnie, I honestly think that you are still in very great danger. I hesitate to speak so plainly to you, but since you have done me the honour to consult me upon your private affairs, I must not remain silent. I fear that almost anything may happen to you – and at almost any moment."

"My God – what on earth do you mean?" Ronnie demanded in a horrified voice, for it was quite obvious to him that Dr. Silla was very much in earnest. Her eyes were fixed upon him with a steady seriousness that was really – considering the subject – nothing less than appalling. "But why – but why – " he stammered. "And from whom? Annie won't do anything; she won't even want to!"

"You are in danger from yourself, Mr. Ronnie," Dr. Silla said quietly, "and because you are too charming! No – please do not laugh; for what I say to you is no laughing matter. To be charming enough – to know how to be nice – if one really *is* nice – that is quite a pleasant thing for everybody, and there is no harm in it. I take it that all human beings would be the better for that knowledge. But you are so *intensely* charming – all your strength goes into it! You use your power up in the effect you make, and none of it is left to carry out your charm! Nobody can afford to appear more pleasant than they really are! It is like walking too far in a high altitude – the mountain air deceives you – you do not feel tired, but suddenly you collapse! One can collapse morally also, from the intoxication of vanity – and then we show what we really are, or what we really feel for this other person who has been up till now agreeably deceived in us! Think to yourself, Mr. Ronnie, what this other person sees then – and what he is liable to do! Believe me, one cannot go on deceiving any intimate! Sooner or later one shows one's true self, and the further apart this self is, from the deception one has used to win the other person's intimacy, the more terrifying is our ordeal, when the truth appears!

"I do not exaggerate, when I tell you that you are in danger. Perhaps you will not come across another human being who would be so careless of herself as to try to murder you! But he or she will certainly pay you out in some other way, very terribly – very dreadfully pay you out! You understand, I am sure, – for you are very intelligent, – *exactly* what I mean?"

Ronnie drew in his breath; for a moment anger seized him, a bitter, furious anger that made him long to tear this cruel woman limb from limb, but the eyes looking into his own held no kindred spark of animosity, on the contrary they were kinder than they had been before.

Dr. Silla looked very sorry for Ronnie, and as if she were anxious to save him from the dangers she foresaw. A naked, sick feeling of fright took slow possession of Ronnie, extinguishing his rage. He felt as if he were being bled white; but not by Dr. Silla. The hand that attacked him was his own. This charm – this terrific compulsion to capture any and every human being, at any price – how often he had felt it swamp him! He was not twenty-five years old without knowing that he had it! But *why* he had it – that he did not know. Nor how he could get rid of it! It was true, what this woman had said. Every intimate relationship Ronnie had ever possessed had tarnished in his eager hands.

At fifteen he had grown tired of his adored and adoring mother. She was the first to fail him. For a long time, Ronnie had continued to hold – and to value — his father's heart. His father was a clergyman; and Ronnie had sung in his choir and read the lessons for him; but in the end because of a series of little college dust-ups, his father had failed him.

Ronnie had been unfortunate earlier than this — because the housemaster at his public school (not Eton, and Ronnie never exactly said he had been to Eton) — was a monster of human depravity. It could hardly be said that his housemaster had failed Ronnie for he had never, from the first, stood high enough to fall. Still Ronnie considered that he had been irretrievably harmed by this medieval brute; had his housemaster been capable of understanding him, what a difference to Ronnie's whole subsequent career this understanding would have made!

Then there were Ronnie's friendships, terrific fiery affairs that went up like rockets and came down like sticks. They had had every quality except that of permanence. His love affairs had been even more ecstatic still and their end more dire, but no girl had ever let him down with the heavy-footed finality of Hilda. Hilda had slashed Ronnie to pieces with her tongue, even before she set out to murder him.

Ronnie looked uncertainly at Dr. Silla. It was disgusting what she had said to him; and still more disgusting what she implied. Should he assume a youthful dignity and simply get up and say: "Well, thank you very much for my good tea, and so on!" and just walk out of the lounge? That would be a lesson to her! But would it? She looked as if she would not mind being left alone. Not that she was hurrying Ronnie off! Not at all, she had lit another cigarette for herself, and she still looked attentive. Her attitude merely told him that he might stay if he liked, but that under no circumstances would she try to keep him. It also told him that it had not been the least use lying to her. He could swagger off, but would not she be swaggering more successfully still, if she just sat there and smiled at his retreating form? For after all, it would be a retreating form.

Ronnie hesitated for a long time, as to what course to take. At last he decided to throw himself upon Dr. Silla's mercy; for he saw that she had mercy; but still to do it in a graceful man-of-the-worldish way.

"Look here," he said, leaning forward with an attractive diffidence, and just touching her wrist with one finger, "isn't it a pretty unreal world that we're all living in? Granted what you say of me is true – what can I do – since I am also, you admit, intelligent – but match it? Isn't it better, and far more fun, to draw a veil of illusion over oneself, and also a little over one's playmates? The truth, you know, isn't always very pretty."

"That," said Dr. Silla reflectively, "was a Shiga culture, that Hilda had in those two tubes. It was a very effective culture from a remarkably potent bacillus. A whole family had already died of it, after great agony, and not at all quickly. It took, I believe, a week. If we had not found out in time, Hilda would have mixed it with your food. It is for you to choose whether or not you prefer deception to truth. Deception too can have consequences that are not very pretty."

Ronnie winced, he could not help showing that she had once more hit him on the raw.

"Mr. Ronnie," the low deep voice began again, "you have another horse in your stall – one that is not vicious, and will carry you very creditably. You are not only so very very charming, but you are also highly intelligent! Will you not tell me how you succeed in your work?"

Another lie was on the tip of Ronnie's tongue, he could easily deceive her here, for how could she guess that he had flunked his last medical? Then he bit his lie back; and said to his own astonishment and also to his own intense relief: "No, I don't succeed really! I *could* work! I mean it's quite true what you say –

I have wits, even my tutor said so – but I don't use them – not like that – I use them to get by with! Exams rather show me up!"

"Well," Dr. Silla said, not at all as if she were blaming him, but as if she were stating a harmless fact, "one can always do that, of course; but then you see the person one is really cheating is oneself. That is what I meant by your danger! You are in danger, I find, of cheating yourself!"

She rose and held out her hand to him. She actually smiled her soothing ripe apricot smile, as if Ronnie were still a pleasant young man highly attractive to her, instead of a poor frightened child, who had been drowning himself in a puddle.

Perhaps she even read the curious image that flashed into Ronnie's mind, for she said consolingly: "You can swim, I suppose?" Ronnie's tongue was too dry for speech, he merely nodded.

"Then you will remember," Dr. Silla said more consolingly still, "what learning to swim was like? One makes, at first, every movement but the right one! And what happens when one has exhausted over and over again, sometimes, all those wrong movements? One finds that by having exhausted them, one has learned to swim! Is not life like that, Mr. Ronnie?

It is out of our mistakes that we become accomplished persons!"

"Please – please sit down again!" Ronnie said passionately. "I'm not like that – not really! It was Hilda who dragged me down – before I knew her I wasn't such a bad fellow! Can't you see what she did to me – what she does still? How she took the heart out of me? I set her intellect free – and she used it against me! Oh, if you only knew how she has tortured me by her deadly criticisms! I couldn't bear it! She undermined, bit by bit, all the strength I had! Dr. Silla, don't go away thinking it was all my fault, or that I'm such a poor low-down rotter – it wouldn't be fair! It wouldn't be true! Think what Hilda did to me!"

"Poor Adam!" Dr. Silla said with a mischievous twinkle in her eyes. "But I'm not God, Mr. Ronnie; I didn't give her to you – and I doubt if God did. Didn't you take her, and by the methods we've just been talking about?" She sat down again however, and lit another cigarette. "How people behave," she told the momentarily silenced Ronnie, "that I have never found interesting! But *why* they behave like it is really useful to know – for then one sees how to cure oneself – and others! Can you not also interest yourself in that? Believe me, Mr. Ronnie, if you fail to understand yourself, you will never understand anyone else! Yes, I know Hilda was angry, and she made a mistake – do not suppose that I at all condone offering any young man, however false, a Shiga bacillus for his breakfast! I am a doctor and I prize life more than anything else in the world. I am also a practical woman and I asked of Hilda, 'Why throw out the baby with the bath?' But of you I must ask something quite different. I must ask, if you wish to avoid being thrown away, why do you dirty your bath water, Mr. Ronnie?" Ronnie threw back his head in haughty displeasure, he was a fastidious person and it had never even occurred to him that his bath water *could* be dirty.

"I believe," Dr. Silla went on slowly, so that he could interrupt her if he liked, at any moment, "I believe that you have not sufficient confidence in yourself, Mr. Ronnie. You have so little that you have to be almost sacred to yourself in order to get on at all! Is it not true that you are afraid of life? You play always the baby. You wish to act, with your charm, as bait for some stronger person, who having swallowed you may then fight your battles for you and protect you! But what a price you must pay for this! How you must suffer! You have just shown me!

And indeed it is not worth your while! Respect yourself enough to be respectable (and you can only respect yourself if you *are* respectable), and then no one will either wish, or *dare*, to do you any harm! Good-bye, for I must really go now – I must telephone to a friend who is awaiting me in Paris that I am now free to join him. Ours is a very fine profession, Mr. Ronnie, and I have a feeling that you will one day make a great success of it!"

She was actually shaking hands with him, as if everything between them was finished when it had only just begun.

Far away, but somehow or other not beyond his reach, Ronnie saw safety. He saw it not as a substance that he might filch from someone else, leaving them his danger in its place; but as something that he might win for himself, without depriving anyone else of it.

He withdrew his rather limp hand from the warm, quick pressure of Dr. Silla's and tried to forget what it would cost to be safe – at his own expense.

Chapter 19

HILDA leaned back in Adrian's business-like little Morris, and watched the neat small world flick softly past her. Houses and trees, fields, and the low lines of cliffs grew vaguer and vaguer.

Hilda felt as if she were recovering from a long and desperate illness, and only wanted to lie still and enjoy the sight of life returning round the corner; but at the back of her mind she knew that she was approaching a fresh ordeal, and must call up her drained strength to meet it. Somehow or other she must find words to blot out Aunt Edith's joy.

Hilda became slowly conscious that the man beside her also had his problem, he was not only concentrating on driving the car.

Adrian was a good driver; he neither took chances that did not belong to him, nor refused those that did; there were no dogs on the road, but if there had been, Hilda thought, he would not have run over them. But it was not of the chances of the changing road that Adrian was thinking.

He wanted to get at something he was too shy to open up; Hilda felt his kindness struggling with his shyness, but she did not know quite how to help him bring out whatever it was that was on his chest. She liked his kindness and his shyness, and she hoped that perhaps, without any effort on her part, he would sooner or later feel that she did; and that this perhaps might be enough, without having to talk about it.

Hilda was too tired to want to find words any more, except those words that she knew she must be ready to say to Aunt Edith.

Adrian waited, hunting about in his mind for the right opening, until they had reached a quiet strip of road, under the downs. "I hope," he said at last awkwardly, "I hope awfully you'll not think any more about that Laboratory business! I—you—it's a curious thing, but as a matter of fact I'm pretty sure there isn't a single human being who hasn't, at one time or another, wanted to get rid of a fellow human being!"

Hilda gave a brief impatient sigh; it was not about

Ronnie she had been thinking. She had not thought of Ronnie once since she had said "Good-bye" to Dr. Silla.

"Perhaps," she said reluctantly, "but most people haven't taken the steps to do it! You see, it's taking the steps that matter – that's what, and quite rightly too, you get hanged for!"

"I shouldn't say 'quite rightly,'" Adrian ventured to contradict her. "Capital punishment is a medieval and barbaric practice; if to take life is wrong, legalized murder is also wrong – you cannot get away from it! It's cowardly too, a sort of sop to make people who haven't been tempted to murder, but who may very well have tempted others to murder them, sleep quietly in their beds! It's true in a sense what you say about it being taking the steps that counts, but still you must remember that those who take the steps take also the risks! They don't satisfy themselves with all that empty spiteful hating that some people fill their lives with – or all that deceptive stuff, either, that goes on under the name of love!"

"That's just it," Hilda acknowledged, wishing he would not make her talk, but suddenly roused to make a contribution towards the conversation, by his last remark. "You're right about love – it is deceptive! But you're wrong if you think it's the having tried to kill that will haunt me. I don't suppose I shall ever take that part quite seriously again. It's a funny thing, but Archer's death blotted it out.

"What *will* haunt me is that I messed up a – relationship, or whatever you like to call a love affair. Dr. Silla showed me that I had! I'm glad she did too, for I suppose that somewhere in the back of my mind I knew that I hadn't quite played the game properly; and until I faced up to it, and saw that I'd helped to make the mess we were in, it would always have been there. What I really wanted to get rid of was what I'd done – only I thought it was the other person! The person I'd done it to, I mean! So I tried to get rid of him!"

Adrian was silent for a long time, as if he were thinking over what Hilda had said, and perhaps agreeing with it.

They had left the sea, and driven into the Downs farther than they needed, Hilda saw, in order to return to Aunt Edith's bungalow; but she said nothing about it, for she would have liked the drive to go on for ever, if only Adrian would not make her think. But Adrian went on making her think. He started again, where they had broken off, as if there had been no silence.

"Deception's horrid, of course," he said meditatively, "but it's not love. That's the mistake people make. Illusion and all attempts at illusion are the exact opposite of love. Love is finding out in another person the sort of things you really like, and can get on with. Of course, the person must have some of the things you don't like as well, but the sooner you learn to see them and discount them, the better. It's those things you like, and swallowing what you don't like, that's love! You've got to have a certain amount of time and sense to find out the difference between a sex desire and a real click; still that's nothing against love, is it?"

"I'm only blaming love because I don't want to blame myself," Hilda said in a low voice. She thought that Adrian had not heard what she said, but after a time he came back to it, and said in the kindest voice Hilda had ever heard, even kinder than Dr. Silla's voice when she had said "Good-bye" to her:

"I'm trying to stop you blaming yourself, but I don't seem very clever at it, do I? I suppose it's because I've another fish to fry as well."

Hilda did not ask Adrian what his other fish was; she thought she might like to find out for herself by and by, when she was alone, but there was no hurry. She simply turned her head, and looked at him. There was light enough still to see Adrian's profile by. It was a face in which pride played a part, without vanity. He wanted, Hilda thought, terribly, not to make mistakes; but there were mistakes he could not make and did not have to worry about; and even those mistakes he *had* made, Hilda thought, he had probably profited by.

"I've *got* to blame myself," Hilda said after a pause, "otherwise I should go on making the same sort of mistake again, shouldn't I? But what you want to help me about is all right! I mean you *have* helped me about it."

Adrian did not ask Hilda what she meant; she saw by his silence that he knew. What he had wanted was to raise her self-respect; and he had raised it. The fact that they had driven far out of their way through the pale chalk Downs, standing low and curved against the colourless pure sky, had raised Hilda's self-respect; since Adrian had shown her by it that he still managed to like her, as a human being, even after she had behaved like the worst of human beings.

"I always wanted to kill my elder brother," Adrian went on after a pause, with a shy friendly laugh. "He had a tiresome habit of always going one better than I could! He won a higher degree; he's got a better job; he married the girl he wanted to marry; and she happened to be the girl I wanted to marry too. But when he had pneumonia a year ago I knew I'd die for him. Funny creatures human beings are, aren't they?"

"Did he die?" Hilda asked, thinking of Archer.

"No," Adrian admitted, "he got better, and I got better too. I found I was quite glad he'd married my sister-in-law, after all! Still, although I no longer have the slightest wish to kill him, I must confess I still have rather a grudge against him!"

"I haven't got even a grudge against Ronnie now," Hilda murmured half to herself, and half to Adrian. "I just feel as if he were a character – not a particularly nice one – that I'd read about in a book. I mean that's the way I feel about him, *by himself*. If I've got to think of what I did to him, then I feel he's real all right! As real as if he were a child I'd kicked downstairs."

Adrian said quickly in a pained voice: "It's the dog you've still got on your mind! Let's stop in Dover and get some bromide for you to take to-night. You mightn't sleep, after that shock!"

Hilda gave a queer little laugh. "All right," she said, "we'll get the bromide! I'll give half of it to Aunt Edith. She's the one that won't sleep!"

Still she felt strangely comforted; it was the way that Adrian had halved her pain by taking it, as it were, into his own being that comforted her. No one had ever really shared Hilda's pain before. Mums had, when she was little, but since Hilda had grown up only – what you might call her broken-leggish pains. Hilda had never told her mother about the other ones. Ronnie – Annie – her father – the friends she had had in school, or made since she had been at work, had always expected Hilda to share their troubles, as well as making her responsible for taking them away. But this strange young man knew by some kind of instinct just when and where Hilda suffered, and seemed to suffer in the same place.

He knew well enough that it was Aunt Edith – it was Archer – it was what Hilda had done to them, because she had been enthralled with her own concerns – that blotted out the lovely softness of the summer night.

The moon came up, a mere silver hoop balancing behind a group of willows, clustering together on a low hillside. Their leaves were already shrivelled on their slender apricot wands. Adrian stopped the car, as if he knew that Hilda would like to watch the way the moon whipped itself out of their frail clutches, into the open darkness of the sky.

After the moon was gone they drove on, in silence into Dover. The little town was full of noise and light; gramophones ground out their half-caste tunes; great ships hooted and whistled; the bustle of the streets made them remember how little they really knew each other. Adrian stopped at three chemists before they found one open for the bromide; and then he drove down to the docks, and stopped the car under the solid shadows of the great ships. It was much quieter there, and Adrian got over feeling that he hardly knew Hilda, and told her with the urgency of an old friend that he thought she ought to take up chemistry and physics. "Typewriting," he said, "is anybody's job." What Hilda should do, was to pass an examination that would enable her to work in a laboratory. She could keep on with her office till she had had time to mug up enough chemistry and physics to pass her tests; it would only take a year or two at most – "An intelligent girl like you," Adrian explained earnestly, "would thoroughly enjoy the extra work; and you'd get more of a future out of science." Hilda at first said "no," but Adrian went on arguing about it, and she had already stopped saying "no" by the time they reached the road that led to the cliffs above Dover.

"Now you go and have your tooth out!" he told her, stopping short at the end of the road that led to the three bungalows. "I'll wait here till I know it's over."

"That's nonsense – please do nothing of the kind!" Hilda told him firmly, but when she had reached the gate, and looked back, she saw that his car was still there.

Aunt Edith met her in the crowded little hall, by the umbrella stand. "My dear, how late you and Archer are!" she exclaimed, before her eyes met Hilda's, and she knew that there was no more Archer.

Hilda did not have to say anything after all. She just looked at Aunt Edith and held out the empty lead.

Aunt Edith said "Oh!" in a strangled, hushed voice, as if she had been bitten by something in church, then she took Hilda in her arms. "My poor dear child," she said tenderly, "my poor dear Hilda!" before Hilda burst into tears. Hilda's tears did Aunt Edith a great deal of good, the more Hilda cried the braver and braver Aunt Edith became.

When Hilda told her, between her sobs, exactly what had happened, Aunt Edith said, "Darling, I believe you risked your life to save him!"

"Well, I did what I could," Hilda admitted between her sobs, "but I killed him first, by forgetting to put him on his lead! My dress tore on the mudguard – I did get a little bang!" Aunt Edith saw that Hilda would have liked it to be an even greater bang, so she made a great deal of fuss about it, and indeed it turned out that Hilda had a severe bruise.

Aunt Edith even tried, later on, to get Hilda to talk about Dr. Silla and the tea-party; but after a time, she went away into the kitchen by herself to get supper.

Hilda suddenly remembered Adrian, and looked out of the front door, although she told herself that he must have driven off ages ago. However, he had not; he saw her standing in the doorway and waved to her; but when Hilda waved from the gate invitingly, Adrian only jumped into the car and drove off. He was really rather a dear, Hilda thought, not to try to come in. He had her London address; but if he had been Ronnie, he would not have driven away until he had supper.

Hilda and Aunt Edith divided the bromide between them, and slept several hours each in consequence.

Waking up, Hilda found, in spite of Archer, was astonishingly nice. She suddenly remembered that it did not matter if bevies of coastguards, or even policemen, met her on the way to the station.

Chapter 20

WHEN Hilda returned home she found herself, tongue-tied and savage, in a net of black conjectures. What had become of Ronnie?

Mr. Fenchurch was sure that the Bolsheviks had removed him, in the same manner that they had once descended upon the Rue Rousselet in Paris, and kidnapped a White Russian general.

"It's come at last," he said several times a day, regarding his two daughters with a smothered fury that showed he held them personally responsible for both incidents, "and now that you see what all this playing with fire leads to. I hope you're satisfied!"

Mrs. Fenchurch's conjectures were both more optimistic and more lenient. She reminded them that

Ronnie had more than once before gone off into the blue without so much as an address or a dropped post-card to signal his return; and yet he *had* returned without a scratch, bringing some of the unflecked azure back with him. Ronnie was always at his most serene when he had been most neglectful. Why therefore *be* upset, even if week-ends did extend themselves into ten days or a fortnight?

Annie, white-faced and shadowy, anxiously scanned the newspapers for motoring accidents, or sudden losses of memory. She had more reason than the rest of the family for supposing that something untoward had happened to Ronnie, since his absence had already broken half a dozen projected engagements.

Hilda was constantly on the brink of telling Annie that Ronnie was safe and that she needn't worry, but it had not yet occurred to her how to do it, without making herself responsible for his absence. After all, it was up to Ronnie to make his own excuses, and no one could tell in advance what particular excuses would be Ronnie's unfettered choice.

Three weeks later, without giving any excuse at all, Ronnie suddenly sent an ex-Etonian friend to bring away his luggage.

No Etonian had ever before been seen in Rostrevor Road (for Ronnie himself wasn't one, however much he liked to think it), so that Mrs. Fenchurch had no idea to what unknown and hostile forces she was opening the front door.

A tall, stringy, hatless young man, dressed with exquisite negligence, stood before her. A rakish scarlet Bugatti at the corner arrested the wondering gaze of all Rostrevor Road, and quite obviously was an essential part of him.

Had Mrs. Fenchurch found herself sliding down a glacier without an icepick, she could not have felt more wholly insecure than this young man intended, and succeeded, in making her feel, with his first freezing glance.

He did not say: "Madam, I suspect you of having two intriguing daughters, who – with your connivance – have entrapped, and then robbed, my inexperienced and innocent young friend. I dare say you will now attempt to blackmail him, but you will have *Me* to deal with! One glance at you overwhelms me with disgust at my young friend's execrable taste in remaining for twenty-four hours under your roof; but it also shows me that you are wholly negligible as an adversary! Give up then your ill-gotten gains or I shall be obliged to call the police!" All he actually said to Mrs. Fenchurch was: "I believe that you have some of Mr. Marsh's things in your house. Will you have the kindness to show me where you keep them, since he will not return." The way he looked down his nose, quite a long one to begin with, the unutterable icy neatness of his whole demeanour, the congealing scorn of his clipped tones, made Mrs. Fenchurch feel as if the young man had been born in a Frigidaire, and brought up on an iceberg by a polar bear.

When she regained what was left of her shuddering breath, and began to ask where and how Ronnie was, he simply brushed past her into the hall, and left her questions in the air – out of which in any coherent form they never succeeded in solidifying, during the rest of his visit.

Annie as it happened was on the stairs, and as he passed her, the young man gave her a look like the blast before an avalanche, a look that simply swept her back into her own bedroom and closed the door upon her. Never had Annie yet had to face a male glance so repugnant and repulsing. "You," the look implied, "are dirt – part of which adheres to the otherwise impeccable shoes of my personal friend (who did at least, though no Etonian, go to Winchester!). But pray don't suppose that *as* dirt you can spread in the direction of mine!"

Hilda, who was in the kitchen, didn't meet the young man at all, she merely heard him moving about overhead – swiftly, and no doubt efficiently, though more accustomed to be packed for, than to pack.

Was he perhaps surprised to find a room so fresh and well ordered, with clothes meticulously folded in suitable places – a room as clean and fresh as the rooms of palaces (even with armies of servants) are seldom kept?

On his way downstairs, dragging with contempt and irritation two large suit-cases with him, the young man called Mr. Fenchurch (who had just come in from the back) "my good man," and told him to open the door, and carry one, if not both, of the suit-cases to his car.

Mr. Fenchurch *did* open the door – his reflex action carried him as far as that; besides he was momentarily speechless, the young man's abrupt and overwhelming arrogance having caught him unawares; but having opened the door he said, with a curious lack of respect for rank and privilege in one of his political views: "You can damned well carry those suit-cases yourself, and don't dare – either you or your friend Ronnie – to darken my doors again!"

After all, as Mr. Fenchurch remarked to Hilda, when she unexpectedly and warmly embraced him for this lapse in his consistency, "an Englishman's home *is* his castle – and neither King nor Commoners have a right to butt in with that tone of voice!"

Mrs. Fenchurch, having by now fully recovered her breath, said a good deal, but Hilda did not wait to hear it. She dashed upstairs to Annie instead. She found her sister lying face downwards on her bed, with her shoulders shaking.

Hilda knelt down and threw her arms round Annie's slender trembling body. "My poor lamb – my poor precious," she whispered in a passion of tenderness and pity. "It wasn't because of you! It's all *me* – and even that young man is in a sense my fault! But I'd have told you sooner Ronnie was safe – only I thought he might have behaved – well, differently! He might have stuck by you! *You* weren't to blame – *you* hadn't cheapened yourself to him, as I did! You see, I thought he might not chuck you – if I just kept quiet and held my tongue! He'll be sorry not to see you again I know – whatever that young man behaved like! Ronnie'll never be sorry not to see *me* again! That's why he didn't come back – he thinks I'm a murderess, and he's not so far wrong either!"

"He thinks *what?*" demanded Annie, sitting bolt upright suddenly, and gazing at Hilda with awestruck eyes. "He thinks *you* – a murderess?"

"Well – yes," Hilda admitted, sliding off her knees

into a more comfortable position on the floor. "That's what I really *am*, Annie! You see, I tried to kill him! I wanted to, anyhow – and I very nearly *did!* It was that foreign lady who stopped me. I don't know now *how* she did it – for I'd got my mind made up. That's why I haven't talked much about that visit to Dover. I told you all about Archer of course, but nothing else. Heaps of other things happened – most of them quite as horrible! Ronnie was there with that nice woman he calls his 'Hag Beauty' – the one he always pretends is in love with him; and borrows money from! Well, I found out she wasn't! She has a blind husband, and isn't like that at all. Ronnie made it all up, because he can't think about a woman without wanting to get the better of her – and pretending that he has, even if he hasn't! With her, he couldn't. That was perfectly plain. I can't think why he goes there – except that it's beautiful. And I dare say they're awfully kind to him, and perhaps he's kind back. I suppose you can't always be as horrid as Ronnie's been to us!

"Perhaps – I don't *know* about this, Annie, but you can't help thinking – perhaps it was partly *me* – and Mum spoiling him so – that made Ronnie so mean! This Mrs. Amondson – I don't think he *could* get the better of her – she'd laugh him out of it! That was the trouble: He got at his worst here with us somehow; and I didn't see any other way of putting a stop to it – except by killing him! I know now, though, that there must be other ways, and even if there weren't – killing Ronnie wasn't my business. But I did *try* everything else first! Everything I knew, I mean!"

Hilda looked up at Annie defensively, but Annie, who had stopped crying, showed neither disapproval nor disgust. She seemed to have lost completely the painful sullenness and suspicion with which she had regarded Hilda during the last few days. Annie looked down at her elder sister with all her old confidence and respect.

"Hilda," she exclaimed breathlessly, "were you actually thinking of killing Ronnie – for my sake?"

Hilda flushed awkwardly. "In a sense I was," she explained. "But perhaps not altogether for your sake, Annie. I got all mixed up. I was furious with him on my own as well! He'd been driving me mad for months! I ought never to have stayed on in the same house with him, after we broke! I see now, I oughtn't to have had that affair with Ronnie at all – I didn't show any sense, from start to finish! But when I saw he was going to let you in for the same game – it was too much for me – I just made up my mind to stop it – even if I had to be hanged for doing it!"

Surprisingly, Annie leaned forward and kissed Hilda; she did it with a conviction she hadn't shown for months. "You stood by me," she said fondly. "You tried to get me out of trouble, Hilda, and – and you *have* got me out of it! And after I was mean to you about Ronnie, too, for I was *really* mean! He'd been your boy – and I oughtn't to have taken him. And I needn't have been so shocked! Tell me everything now – I shan't ever be shocked with you again, not whatever you do!"

Hilda told her everything, sitting on the floor still, but with her head propped against Annie's knee; while Annie, as usual supported by pillows, laid one hand affectionately upon Hilda's thick wavy hair, and listened intently. No one would ever hear again what Hilda told Annie; her words were not trying to hide anything behind them; and Annie understood, not because she was particularly clever at understanding, but because they *were* sisters and long ago had passed the barriers of self-protection and strangeness that separate those of another blood. The same breast had fed them, the same firm hand had very occasionally and reluctantly spanked them; until they died they would be young to each other.

Annie did not listen only to what Hilda said, she listened to what Hilda *meant*. All the silly, generous, angry, muddle-headed, tender, savage blunders Hilda had plunged into – from Ronnie's first kiss to that incredible hour in the Laboratory when she had taken, so cleverly and so unwisely, those two tiny tubes that might have brought upon the little house in Rostrevor Road the pack of the Press, – the pressure of the Law, – the frightful penalty of a frightful crime, – were crystal-clear to Annie, as clear as if she had made each blunder herself. All the pitiful, pitiless horrors of Hilda's mind disclosed themselves to her sister in the summer dusk; and disclosing them, Hilda got rid of them for ever.

When Hilda had finished unpacking the truth of her heart, Annie bent over and kissed her again. She held Hilda close, as if her thin, rather powerless arms could protect that strong and passionate elder sister against the whole blind, inexorable, dangerous world.

"It's all *right*, Hilda," Annie whispered into the heavy silence. "It's all right! I mean I shan't mind now – not ever – about Ronnie! I never did as much as you think, that's why I didn't understand what you told me. I wouldn't have been all cross and shocked over it, if I'd cared more myself! I dare say I *should* have given in to him though, sooner or later, if you hadn't saved me! It's not so easy always saying 'no' to a man in the same house! And Ronnie was such a one for having his own way. He gave me ever such good times, too. Better than anyone else ever has! He could be terribly sweet to you – Ronnie! But in a way I never liked him as much as a *real* man, for he isn't one! I mean he doesn't always behave like one, does he? Ronnie isn't as silly, and he isn't as *decent* as a real man! I've known lots of men – better than you have perhaps, Hilda – because I'm not so clever, and so they don't mind showing me what they're really like. They're afraid of you! The men I mean were different from Ronnie. They hadn't that Pansy touch! They'd have come back themselves to pack their own things!"

"Yes," Hilda whispered. "Yes – I see what you mean. I suppose they would!"

"That man," Annie went on earnestly and anxiously, "the one in the white coat in the Laboratory, who came down to Dover afterwards for the – the tubes – was he different – different that way, I mean – from Ronnie?"

"Yes," Hilda admitted without looking up; "and he's been to my office once or twice since. He took me out to lunch; but he hasn't said anything, Annie – only lent me some books! I haven't thought about him seriously – yet."

"Well, that's all right then," said Annie in a relieved voice, as if she were now the elder sister instead of Hilda. "If he's different, I mean, from Ronnie. He *needn't* say things – that's what I mean – the real ones don't! You *know* what they mean – and they *know* what you mean! That's the way it works."

"Now then, you girls . . ." Mrs. Fenchurch's voice, once more restored to its usual cheerfulness, boomed up the stairs. "Stop all that chattering! And come down to your suppers – while the kippers are hot."

THE END